five-minute
mysteries

five-minute
mysteries

a further
36
cases
of
murder
and
mayhem
for
you
to
solve

4

ken weber

FIREFLY BOOKS

A FIREFLY BOOK

Published by Firefly Books Ltd., 2004

First Printing 2004

National Library of Canada Cataloguing in Publication

Weber, K. J. (Kenneth Jerome), 1940-
Five-minute mysteries 4 / Ken Weber.
Previously titled: Further five minute mysteries.
ISBN 1-55297-866-4
1. Detective and mystery stories, Canadian (English)
2. Literary recreations. 3. Puzzles. I. Title.
GV1507.D4W426 2004   793.73   C2003-905896-4

Published in Canada in 2004 by
Firefly Books Ltd.
66 Leek Crescent
Richmond Hill, Ontario L4B 1H1

Design: HotHouse Canada
Printed and bound in Canada by Friesens, Altona, Manitoba

To Eric and Doris Cuddon,
from whom I learned a great deal

Unsolved Cases

Memorandum

To: ALL MYSTERY BUFFS
From: the author

Mystery buffs know there are only two kinds of people in the world: those that love mysteries and, well, that other kind. A tiny majority, the latter are, and that's a good thing because they are missing something unique. For only in mysteries can a reader get a charge out of winning or losing.

It works like this. Nothing gives mystery buffs more satisfaction than getting ahead in a story and beating the writer to the punch. They get a special charge out of combining logic, analysis, intuition and insight so that before they turn the last page, they already have the problem solved. Yet – and this is what sets mystery lovers apart – nothing thrills them more than when the mystery defeats them, when they turn the last page and find a surprise waiting, something they'd missed.

In this, the fourth installment of the series, mystery lovers get no less than thirty–six shots at the fun of winning or losing, in a set of wildly different stories. Every mystery in the book is set up for the reader to solve. At the end of each mystery there is a question: **Who did...?** or **What did...?** or **It seems the thief made a mistake. How could...?** Like that.

There's great variety. The settings range from city to country, from soccer field to fourteenth century church, and from a U.N. meeting room to a hardware store to a sinking ship in Halifax harbor. You'll encounter veteran detectives, medical examiners, special agents, a drug enforcement officer and crime-scene investigators.

There's also variety in the level of challenge. As turn the pages of **Five-minute Mysteries 4**, you'll notice one, two or three symbols – a fingerprint – at the beginning of each story. The number of fingerprints suggests how easy or difficult the mystery is, one being easy, two being a little harder, and three, difficult. (Or, perhaps more accurately, how easy or difficult each one seems to me.) But don't let the ratings stop you from enjoying all the mysteries! One that I rate "difficult" might be an open-and-shut case for you, while you might be utterly stumped by one I've rated "easy." Try them all.

Finally, all the solutions are at the back of the book, so you can prove you're a winner or, once in a while, get a kick out of losing. Either way, enjoy.

1

A Decision at Rattlesnake Point

The cable screamed over the large pulley at the end of the mobile crane, launching a massive assault on the morning quiet. The arm of the crane was fully extended to reach over the brow of Rattlesnake Point, for the body had to come up from two hundred feet below. It was the distance more than the weight that made the equipment work so hard.

As he talked to Trevor Hawkes, the young doctor from the medical examiner's office watched the big machine with a wary eye. Perry Provato had ridden down and then back up via the crane within the past hour, and he was not at all impressed by what he saw, now that he was watching from the top.

"It's like I said, Trevor," he pointed sideways with his thumb at the body that was now coming over the edge of the cliff. Trussed up in a rescue basket, it bounced and swayed at the end of the cable like some macabre yo–yo that had got stuck on the way to the spool. "Like I said, I might do a bit better at the morgue this afternoon, but I'll take bets that the death took place six to eight hours ago."

Trevor nodded and looked at his watch. "So ... 'tween one and three a.m. Makes sense." He motioned to the crane operator and then pointed to a clear spot beside the guardrail. "Highway patrol reported the car at, let's see, 4:46. Then ... "

He waved frantically at the crane operator. "No! No! This side! Over here!" he yelled, pointing with both arms to the spot beside the rail.

"So," he said, his voice returning immediately to normal, "first light was 5:20. Patrol confirmed a body down in the scrub about ten minutes after that. And you went down, what? About eight o'clock. An hour ago, right?"

"Yeah, eight," Perry replied. "Never done that before. Go down on a cable, I mean. Can't say I want to again either! You just stand on the big grab hook and hang on! I mean, even the dead guy gets strapped into a basket.

"And what a mess when I got down there! He's a big guy. Not lanky like you, but a big one. Just think of the acceleration by the time he hit!"

Perry shook his head; his adrenaline was still pumping. "I remember this sicko physics teacher we had in high school. Liked to give us problems with falling bodies. She should try this one!"

Trevor looked at the body, lying finally where he had directed. Despite Perry's comment, it appeared remarkably intact. After a two-hundred-foot fall, all the parts were still there. In fact the face was almost unscathed. Only the big belly seemed pushed oddly to one side, and the suspenders on that side had come off. Trevor could see that the neck was broken, likely the spine, too, in several places.

"One thing, Perry, before you go. In your, uh, your uh, uh ... " Trevor was trying to find the right word. Perry was so young. He settled on *"experience,"* anyway. "In your experience, uh ... well, there's a note on the driver's seat in the car there." He knew that Perry was looking at the silver-gray Lincoln Town Car behind them. It was parked in perfect parallel on the verge between the road and the guardrail. "Can't be sure, of course, till we go inside, but my guess is it's a suicide note. Now, what makes a guy do himself in like that when there's ...?"

"You mean," Perry took the lead, "why didn't he just let the car run and go to sleep? Or overdose? Or something softer like that? I dunno. I guess some of them just want to be more dramatic. I know that some jumpers do it because they really want to punish themselves. But it's a lot quicker the way he did it! Then there's always the ... "

The rest of what Perry had to say was erased by the scream of the cable. Both men looked to see Trevor's rookie partner, Ashlynne Walmsley, on her way over the brow of Rattlesnake Point. Unlike the other passengers so far, it was clear she was enjoying herself completely. Ashlynne waved a camera at Trevor as soon as the operator set her down.

"Lots of shots," she said. "Covered everything."

Trevor pointed to the body. "Get a couple there," he said, "then the car from several angles. And ... just a minute!" He knelt beside the body. "Make sure you witness this." He patted the dead man's pockets and then reached into one of them and extracted a small ring of keys. "Just in case some jackass lawyer ever wants to know in court where we got these."

"Trust me," Ashlynne said and began snapping shots of the car.

Trevor, meanwhile, waved goodbye to the retreating Perry and went to the driver's door of the Lincoln. He inserted a key and turned it sharply. All four door-locks popped open simultaneously, along with – to his complete surprise – the trunk lid. He reached for the door handle, then shrugged and went to the back of the car instead. Except for a CD player and a small rack of discs, the cavernous trunk was empty and very clean. With his pen, Trevor spread the discs apart and craned his neck to read the titles, only to bump into Ashlynne who was peering over his shoulder.

"George Strait, Randy Travis, Dolly Parton," she read aloud. "Reba McEntire. All country. Well, he's consistent anyway. Kitty Wells! Who's Kitty Wells?"

The question made Trevor feel his age so he ignored it. "Time to go inside," he said. "There's nothing here. You go to the passenger side and open up. Just witness what I do. I got a funny feeling we're going to have to explain a lot about this one."

"You mean," Ashlynne asked, "you think it's fishy that a guy would park his car so neat if he's going to jump? And lock it, too? And take the keys?"

Trevor didn't answer. He simply walked around to the driver's door and opened it after Ashlynne had done as she was instructed. The paper on the seat was of a standard memo-pad size. Again using his pen, Trevor turned it over. It was a note. It said simply:

Try to get me *now*.

A.

"Want my flashlight?" Ashlynne asked when she saw Trevor tilt up the steering column and bend himself in to look under the seat.

He just shook his head.

"Then is it okay if I see where the radio stations are pre-set? And, uh, like, Trevor ... shouldn't the fingerprint people be here?"

Trevor Hawkes maneuvered himself back out of the car and stretched his long frame. He looked over at the crane operator who had sidled as close as he dared to the body.

"Good thinking on the radio stations," he said finally. "And yeah, you're right. Let's give the forensic bunch their shot. There won't be any prints though. Whoever murdered this guy isn't that dumb."

?

What has finally convinced Trevor Hawkes that this is a murder case?

Solution on page 177

2

Something Suspicious in the Harbor

Sue Meisner brought both oars forward into the little rowboat and drifted until the boat bumped against the huge freighter. It was especially dark down here on the water between the two big ocean-going ships. She felt as though she were in a tunnel, with the superstructure of *The Christopher Thomas* looming over her and the even bigger Russian ship alongside, completing the arch. Still there was enough light from the city to see the mark from early this morning, the little paint scrape where Sue had bumped against *The Christopher Thomas* the first time.

That had been with the police boat though, and Sue had been acting officially, as a constable with the Metropolitan Toronto Police marine unit. However, there was nothing official about this trip. It was anything but. She was in restricted waters to boot. Tiny, privately operated rowboats were not welcome in the main channel of Toronto harbor, and Sue knew if she were caught there, it would be hard to imagine what would be worse: her embarrassment or Inspector Braemore's wrath.

That was why, at sunset, she had taken the ferry from the city over to Ward's Island, collected the rowboat, and then pulled her way across the channel in the dark. By staying close to the piers along Cherry Street, she'd reached *The Christopher Thomas* undetected. So far anyway.

Sue shifted on the seat to relieve her sore back. The movement caused the little craft to rock, and it banged hard into the side of the freighter. The rowboat was aluminum, and to her, the sound in the tunnel between the two larger vessels was like a gunshot. But she knew it wouldn't be heard on deck. With the racket up there and in the hold, especially from the noisy diesels powering the loading winches, there wasn't a chance even for normal conversation, let alone picking up a sound from the surface of the water.

The crew of *The Christopher Thomas* had been loading big containers full of automobile engines for several hours already when Sue and her partner had made their official visit that morning. The two officers were responding to a tip. Sue had taken the call herself right after coming on duty.

"Something crooked in the harbor," the caller had said. "On *The Christopher Thomas* and maybe that Russian one beside her – the *Potemkin* something. You people should go check." Then the caller had hung up.

Inspector Braemore had not been very impressed. It was his opinion that some disgruntled sailor wanted to harass the shipowners and was using the police to do it. And Sue's visit this morning, if anything, seemed to confirm that, for they'd seen nothing amiss. She and her partner had circled the ship inside and outside. There were no safety violations, no evidence of contraband, not even a suggestion of drug use in the crew's quarters. *The Christopher Thomas* appeared to be just a freighter being filled with cargo by a busy crew that did not want two police officers getting in their way.

It was Inspector Braemore's I-told-you-so expression that had got

Sue's dander up. It explained why, later in her shift, she had stood on the nearby ferry docks for half an hour and watched the loading through binoculars, and why she'd checked the ship's papers twice with the harbormaster. And it also explained – or so she told herself – why sore back and all, she was sitting in a tiny rowboat in the smelly darkness of Toronto harbor long after sunset.

"Well," she said out loud, "at least, it's paid off. At least now I *know* there is certainly something crooked going on. Tomorrow morning there's going to be another inspection so we can find out just what it is!"

What has led Sue Meisner to the conclusion that something crooked is going on aboard *The Christopher Thomas?*

Solution on page 178

In Search of Answers

Every window in the little studio was open as wide as possible in a vain attempt to catch whatever tired breeze might limp by from time to time. Inside, however, this arrangement produced no results. The air in the place had been hot, wet and motionless all day. Still, at least one of Celeste Wyman's questions was answered: namely, why had Virgil Powys left every window – and the door, too – wide open when he supposedly dashed back to his house? In this heat wave, it made sense. No one was closing windows these days.

There was an answer, too, for another of Celeste's questions. Why wasn't the place air conditioned? By visiting the studio personally, by actually coming to the scene of the crime, so to speak, Celeste could see that an air conditioner would be intolerable. Too noisy. And it would box the place in. One of the studio's charms was that, despite the tight quarters, the number of windows created an impression of space. Powys claimed he had claustrophobia. Celeste certainly didn't, but she could sense what the effects would be if the sight lines were blocked.

She sat down at the table that served as a desk and looked out the large window across the room. Beyond it, over the alley and on the other side of a line of mature oak trees, traffic from Bronson Avenue superimposed its noise over the buzz and beep and mutter of the computers to her right. Side by side, on a counter that ran the length of the one wall without a window, sat a Power Mac G5, and beside it, a much more modest laptop. Celeste leaned a little closer to the G5. Eight gigabytes of memory, she figured. Dual 2GHZ processors. Powerful. A lot more powerful than its immediate neighbor.

The machinery made a sharp contrast to the Chippendale repro-duction table at which she was sitting, but both the table and counter shared the disarray of the studio. Stashed in every available space on the counter was a flotsam of envelopes jammed with mate-rial, the lot held in place by a Gordian knot of wires and cables and power bars that only an original installer could ever untie. On the nearest edge of the table, pens spilled out of a pewter beer stein and trailed across to a pewter envelope holder lying empty on its side. On the left edge, irregular stacks of medical reference texts were interspersed with piles of dictionaries and manuals.

Celeste lifted a heavy metal stapler from the pile of papers on the crowded working surface in front of her. The first page, and then the second, the third, and then the fourth, when she looked further, answered yet another question. Powys was obviously one of those types who worked things out on paper first and only then went to the keyboard. It was not what she would have expected. Someone with his expertise, his passion for computers, seemed more likely to work "cold," right on the keyboard with no intermediate steps.

Virgil Powys had a reputation as a computer wunderkind. He'd started with IBM three years ago, and after two revolutionary patents, jumped to Apple for six months and then to Dell for two before going freelance. But he wasn't doing well at freelancing. He was brilliant but erratic; he needed the discipline of an organization around him, but with his reputation for instability no one would touch him anymore. Nevertheless, when Celeste's company, Hygiolic Incorporated, retained him six weeks ago, they thought they'd made a steal. This morning, "steal" suddenly had a whole new meaning.

Celeste Wyman was Director of Research at Hygiolic. It was a company specializing in the development and production of highly advanced and complicated drugs and medicines. For months the company had been on the verge of a historic medical breakthrough. By means of computer models, they had developed – theoretically – a vaccine to protect against common cold viruses. The trouble was no one could put all the strands together; there wasn't anybody in Celeste's department who could do it. And the board of directors had so severely limited access to the models for security reasons, that, in effect, Hygiolic had been going nowhere with what could be the biggest thing since the Salk vaccine.

Yesterday, Powys had called to say he'd done it. This morning he called again, this time to say he thought the work might have been pirated, that while he'd been out for just minutes, someone had been into the studio and into the program.

Celeste leaned back in the chair and stretched, idly running both index fingers against the flyscreen behind her. There were so many questions. Should she call the police? Not yet. Find out more first. Is it possible that Powys himself was stealing the program? That this whole break-in thing was a red herring? Not likely. It would be too hard for him to sell it. Oh, there were companies that would grab it first chance. But from Powys? No. Too easy to trace.

She leaned forward again, and put her elbows on the table. Did whoever had been into the system actually steal Hygiolic's big discovery? Yes. At the very least that had to be assumed. Espionage in medical research is as vicious as in warfare.

But then there were the truly niggling questions. Was Virgil

Powys in cahoots with whoever did the pirating? Why, especially if he had put audit controls in the system that could tell him if someone had been into it, had he not encrypted the data? Used code? Powys's explanation was that Hygiolic was pushing so hard for results that using an encryption scheme good enough to protect against even a run-of-the-mill hacker would have slowed him right down. Reasonable enough, Celeste knew; she had been one of the ones pushing.

But then, at the very least, why hadn't he protected his system with a password? The answer to that was on the wall. For the third or fourth time in the past half hour, Celeste looked up at the wall above the laptop. In large block letters she could see "HYGISNEEZE" written on the wallpaper with a felt-tipped pen. She shook her head. He had used a password all right! But then, hanging it out for all to see was something she did herself. So did others in her department. Not on the wallpaper though.

A noise from behind her made Celeste turn. Through the open door she could see Sean, her assistant, leaving the back door of the house and making his way across the lawn to the shed where Powys had built the studio. She counted Sean's steps: twenty-five. About twenty seconds, she calculated. Another ten to come up the stairs. Powys had said he'd gone back to the house to go to the bathroom, so that would be about thirty seconds each way. Allow, say, five minutes in the bathroom. Then he got a phone call. Long distance, he'd said, so that would be easy to verify. The call took about five minutes, supposedly, so according to Powys, he was out of the studio for ten or eleven minutes. Enough time for a pirate to dash in and copy everything? No, not at all, no matter how good. Not even if he knew where to go and how to get in.

So, was Virgil Powys out of the studio for longer than he had said he was? No doubt about it. And was he out for a longer time because he had arranged to be? Well, Celeste thought, maybe it is indeed time to involve the police. They're probably better at finding out that kind of information. At least she knew that Powys needed to be questioned.

Why is Celeste Wyman certain that Virgil Powys was out of the studio for longer than the time he claimed to be?

Solution on page 179

4

A Single Shot in the Chest

Brian Breton held his tongue as long as he could.

"For heaven's sake, Roly!" he finally blurted. "Doesn't it bother you to be playing with evidence like that?"

Roly Coyne lowered the binoculars for just a second, looked at them as though he were seeing them for the first time, and then put them back to his eyes.

"C'mon," he said. "What do you mean *evidence?* Who cares! This case is open and shut. At least as far as you're concerned. You got a body. You got a shooter. You got a confession. What more do you want? This case is, like *closed*. I mean, *shut!* 'Sides, that's the ten o'clock class across the street there. I'll bet half the guys in our building are doing what I'm doing right now."

What Roly Coyne was doing, along with – according to him – half the guys in the building, was focusing a pair of binoculars on an aerobics class across the street from the morgue.

"You see, this ten o'clock bunch," Roly went on with unconcealed delight, "it's the one with all the chicks from the college up the street."

For the first time since Brian Breton had slipped into the office five minutes ago, Roly turned his back to the window and faced him. "Here, see for yourself."

He handed the binoculars to Brian. "C'mon, take a look!" he insisted. "You never seen a spandex parade like this! Not over in the coroner's office anyway!"

"Aw, Roly, get off it!" Brian was annoyed. "It's bad enough being here without your juvenile nonsense." He used the opportunity to take the binoculars out of Roly's hand. "Besides, these are no good to someone like me, with glasses, without those little rubber cups on the eyepieces. Anyway, forget this and let's get down to the cooler. I want to get this over with."

Roly sighed. "Okay, Breton." He swiveled back to the window for one final, drooling stare. "You want to take any *terribly important evidence* down with us?" Without taking his eyes off the window he waved his hand vaguely at a table in the corner to his right. "It's all over there."

Brian had perused the evidence before, while Roly was studying aerobics. In addition to the binoculars Roly was using, there was a well-worn pocketknife with one of the blades broken off, a few coins, some wooden matches, a very dirty handkerchief, three fence staples, a bent nail, and – this one really caught Brian's eye – a World War I issue Ross rifle with the name MANOTIK burned crudely into the wooden butt.

"No," he said to Roly. "The evidence can stay here so you have something to play with when the aerobics class is over. Now let's go!"

Roly swiveled frontwards again. "All right, all right." Reluctantly he got to his feet. "Actually, this one shouldn't be so bad for you. Just your average dead body with a hole in the chest. I don't see why it always makes you sweat so. You don't have to kiss him! Anyway, you should have done this before I washed old Manotik. I bet he never had a bath in twenty years! Did he *stink* or what!"

"Roly! Just let's go." Already Brian was feeling sick to his stomach.

After thirty years as an investigator with the coroner's office, he still had nightmares after a visit to the cooler, the refrigerated room full of slabs in sliding cabinet drawers where bodies were stored. Whenever he could, Brian ducked out of his obligation to examine cadavers, and in the case of old Manotik he was very tempted.

Manotik was a hermit who, for as long as anyone could remember, had lived in a swamp north of the city. The problem was, he was a squatter. Manotik had never owned the swamp. Three years ago, a company called Nucleonics Inc. had moved in, drained off all the water, built a complex of modern buildings, then surrounded the property with a huge chain-link fence and patrolled it twenty-four hours a day with armed guards. In a humanitarian gesture it soon regretted, Nucleonics granted Manotik a small piece of land next to the fence. It was from this base that the old man launched his campaign of harassment. At least the company *believed* it was the old man. His guilt had never been established.

At first, the problems were annoying but manageable. The Nucleonics property was plagued in turn by an infestation of snakes, then rats, and then skunks. But one night a section of fence was dynamited. A week later it happened again. Then the worst step of all: on six different occasions over the past two months, rifle bullets had winged through the windows of the Nucleonics executive suites. When a secretary was badly cut by flying glass, the company doubled the guard. It was one of the new guards who had shot the old man.

"His statement is pretty simple, isn't it? The guard's, I mean." Roly was repeating what Brian already knew as the elevator creaked its way down to the cooler. "He sees the old guy at the fence with the rifle poked through it, sorta hangin' there in the chain link. But shoulder level. And he's got those binoculars focused on the exec suite. The guard shouts at Manotik and the old guy grabs the rifle, so boom! The guard offs him. I'd say the plea'll be self-defense."

Brian wasn't listening. They had crossed the short hallway into the cooler and he was bracing himself. Roly, meanwhile, seemed to get cheerier.

"Number 42," he said, "right here." He rolled out the slab and grabbed a corner of the cover sheet. "And now! For your viewing pleasure ... Ta-da!"

Brian gagged. "God, Roly," he muttered, then forced himself to look at the scrawny white form that had once been Xavier Manotik. Roly was right about the bullet wound, an almost harmless looking hole in the chest. The rest of the body looked so clean and untouched. So did the face. Well, almost. Roly may have scrubbed it, but years of dirt still marked the ridges on the old man's forehead and darkened the cleft in his chin. Only the nose seemed really clean. It was a long, thin nose with callused indentations on both sides of the bridge, and creases leading down from it toward the mouth, the kind of creases that come from years of frowning.

Brian leaned closer to see the stubble on the old man's cheeks. Despite his distaste for this routine, he never failed to be fascinated by the fact that body hair continued to grow after death.

"Hey, you startin' to like this or something?" Roly's voice intruded. "Seen enough or what?" Roly wanted to get back to the aerobics class. "Let's go up and you can sign off."

"Not yet, Roly. Not yet," Brian replied. "There's something about that guard's story that smells as bad as this place does."

"What do you mean?" Roly asked.

?

What does Brian Breton mean? What's wrong with the guard's story?

Solution on page 179

5

The Case of the Stolen
Stamp Collection

In the doorway of Mika Fleck's office stood a very nervous young man in a blue delivery uniform. Miles Bender was waiting to be summoned, and he wasn't the least bit comfortable about the idea.

Mika's opening statement didn't help either. "Come in here and sit down, young man," she said without looking up. "For heaven's sake, you're going to wear out the rug with your fidgeting."

Miles shuffled across the floor to the only chair that was empty of books and files and all the paraphernalia of an extremely busy office. "It didn't get there, did it?" he said as he sat down. "The shipment. Like, the stamps?"

Mika looked over the top of her half-glasses, freezing Miles Bender in mid-squirm. "No," she said. "It did not. The first bonded shipment that Acceleration Courier Service has ever failed to deliver." She pushed up her glasses and looked through them. It didn't make Bender feel any more relaxed. "And I don't suppose you're surprised to know that collection is worth over half a million dollars. That's why we had a police escort."

"I know it was valuable." For the first time, Miles Bender stopped squirming. "I know that. But how can you blame *me* if the cops stole it. I mean – they looked like cops anyway."

Mika spread her hands on the desk and spoke more softly. "Okay. Let's go through it again. You say two policemen took the stamps. Just like that."

"Not just like that." Miles was beginning to whine in spite of Mika's obvious attempt to be more gentle with him. "I mean, they were cops! Look, it was standard procedure. All the way to the border, like, there were these two Vancouver city cops, one in front and one in back just the way we're supposed to do it. And at the border the two American cops took over, the ones from Bellingham. Motorcycle cops."

Miles Bender was becoming more confident as he sensed his side of the story was finally being listened to. He leaned forward in the chair. "I mean, there was no reason to be suspicious; you wouldn't have been either. They had real police bikes. Real uniforms – the boots, the gloves, the sunglasses, everything!"

Mika opened her mouth to speak, but Miles kept talking. "I mean they even *acted* like motorcycle cops. You know, sort of strutty and cocky and ..."

"According to this report," Mika broke in, "you got a good look at them."

Miles took a deep breath. "At *one* of them, yeah. When we stopped on the highway and they made me get out. The one that put his bike in the van and, like, got in to drive, he got pretty close."

"According to your description," Mika said, "he is about your height, but heavier. Bit of a beer belly. Blue eyes and a reddish mustache. Maybe 35 to 40 years old."

"Yeah!" Miles Bender was enthusiastic in his agreement. "And the cut, the nick on his cheek? They got that on the report there? Like maybe he cut himself shaving?"

Mika nodded and then looked up from the report. "And you say all this took only a couple of minutes. They stopped. You stopped. They ordered you out, and then one of them put his bike in the van, and they took off leaving you at the side of the road."

"Exactly! That's it exactly!" Miles was excited now. "I mean, like, by this time I know they're not cops but, I mean, like, what am I gonna do?"

Mika cleared her throat. She was looking over the top of her glasses again. "For one," she said, "you're going to tell us where they took the stamps. Depending on how well you do that, we'll work out the next steps later."

?

Why is Mika Fleck suspicious of Miles Bender?

Solution on page 180

Not Your Average Hardware Store

"So you think that's why we were handed this one?" Gordon Pape's question was rhetorical. He really didn't expect an answer but got one anyway.

"Figure it," Hugh Furneaux said. "Why else would the agency bring us this far north? It can't be any other reason. They've more than enough bodies up here for this kind of work."

"This kind of work," on this particular morning, was a repossession. Gordon Pape and Hugh Furneaux worked for SIMM Resolutions, a collection agency. "Field operatives," they were called in the agency's pretentious terminology, the ones who actually went out to face the locked doors, the insults, the angry dogs, the tears, even on occasion – and by far the most disturbing – sad, silent acceptance. All in order to repossess unpaid merchandise.

"My God. Look at it!" Hugh Furneaux exclaimed. "He must be a character all right."

The two operatives had pulled off the road to park in front of an ugly cement-block building. Its large yellow and black sign proclaimed it to be:

"A Real Man's Hardware Store."

Hugh scanned the shopworn banners in the display windows that flanked the front door. "Hard to believe there aren't some feminists out picketing here," he said. "I could see their point, too!"

The banners, all of them as dusty as the goods in the display windows, each supported Wilfrid Norman's idea of what a *real* hardware store must be, or a real *man's* hardware store at any rate.

"Real Men Don't Buy Teacups," one said.

Another offered:

"You Want Seven of Something? Ask Us!"

And directly underneath:

"No Pre-Packaging! We Sell You What You Want!"

Still another announced:

"If We Ain't Got It, Then It Ain't Hardware!"

The "ware" had partly torn off from the end of the last banner and hung away from its host sentence at an awkward angle.

"You know," Hugh observed to his partner, "it may not just be that we're strangers. This guy could be very hard-nosed. Did you see the shepherd running loose out back in the storage area? I'll bet he didn't come with a 'Good with Children' guarantee. Wonder if there's any of those loose inside?"

Gordon Pape was about to reply but then paused. He was looking at the Christmas lights that hung from the fluorescent fixtures just behind the windows. In mid-July. Apparently Wilfrid Norman's sole concession to the festive season was to plug and unplug an extension cord.

"I was here once," he said absently. "Needed a new handle for my splitting maul up at the cottage."

"Your *what?*" For the first time since they'd pulled in, Hugh took his eyes off the front of Norman's hardware store and looked directly at Gordon.

"A spli ... Never mind. Not important," Gordon said. "The point is, the guy had one here. In stock. Actually he had about half a dozen! You just don't buy that kind of thing in a typical hardware store anymore. That's one of those crummy special orders that takes forever and gets surcharged to boot, all because some bean counter has told the owner his inventory has to roll over a certain number of times a year."

"And the whole place is like that," Gordon continued. "Full of everything you'd never get anywhere else. It's dirty and it's dusty and it's scattered all over the store. There's bins, barrels, shelves. Don't know how anybody can find anything, but they do. Well, anyway, he does. Norman, I mean." He paused reflectively for a moment. "It's really your good old-fashioned hardware store. Everybody for miles around knows it."

"That's what I meant about why we were asked to do this," Hugh commented. "All the SIMM people up here must know him. That's why we're here to pick up – what is it anyway? It's a computer isn't it?" He reached into the back seat for a clipboard. "Yeah. Kirznet Cash Flow Control System."

He looked out at the display windows again. "Somehow it just doesn't seem to fit in there, does it?"

Gordon chuckled. "Probably why he hasn't paid for it."

"Well, pay or not," Hugh opened the car door, "let's get it over with." He was halfway out the door and then sat down again. "By the way, I make it 9:15. Is that what you've got? Awfully late for an old-fashioned hardware store to still be closed."

"That's true," Gordon replied, a note of concern in his voice.

The two men got out and stood beside their car to take in a wider view. The area was very quiet. There was no one else around.

The "Real Man's Hardware Store" had no sidewalk in front of it, just a small parking lot, empty this morning. There were no adjacent stores either; the building was separated from the edge of town by a small field.

"This isn't a holiday or something, is it?" Hugh looked at Gordon as they approached the front door. "Don't they have a half-holiday or something like that in these little towns when everybody closes."

"Not in the morning," Gordon said, somewhat distractedly for they'd reached the door and it was definitely locked.

"Wow! Look at that latch!" Hugh said. "This has to be the last store in the country with a thumb la ... Oh, oh! Look there."

"I see it – him," Gordon answered.

On the floor inside, just a few steps from the door, the body of a man lay face down at an angle slightly oblique to the door. Hugh and Gordon moved to the display windows on either side so they could peer in.

The body was that of a man at the far end of middle age. They could see white hair protruding over the edge of a baseball cap, some of the tufts leading to the back of his lined neck. He wore a red smock, the kind one might normally expect on a hardware store clerk.

The position of the body seemed peculiar. It lay in a very wide pool of blood that seemed to have congealed at the edges now. The man's legs were crossed at the ankles as though he had tripped himself and fallen that way. One hand, his left, was in the pocket of his shiny brown pants. The other was in the small of his back, palm upward. In the wan light from the fluorescents left on for night-time security, both Hugh and Gordon noted its soft, clean, white-ness in contrast to the menace just above it. For there, inches above the hand, thrust deep into the man's back, was a black-handled knife, a multi-purpose sportsman's knife, probably one from the store. It appeared as though the victim's last living effort had been to try to pull it out.

Neither Hugh nor Gordon felt an urge to rush. There was no question the man was dead and had been for some time.

"I'll call," Hugh said, pulling himself back from the scene. "Do they have 911 here?"

"They must," Gordon replied. "Wouldn't matter anyway. Everybody knows Wilfrid Norman's place."

"Sure, but that's not Wilfrid Norman," Hugh said over his shoulder on the way to the car and the cellular phone.

? Gordon Pape has been to Wilfrid Norman's store before, and might recognize the hardware man, but how does Hugh Furneaux know that the dead man is not Wilfrid Norman?

Solution on page 180

7

Murder at 249 Hanover Street

As she pulled over to the curb, Janet Dexel cocked her head a little closer to the portable radio on the seat beside her.

"The wettest first day of October since records were started in 1826," the announcer was saying, "and the outlook for the next several days is more of the same."

Janet snapped off the radio and peered almost gloomily across the sidewalk at 249 Hanover Street. "A perfectly miserable day," she said out loud to herself, "and now a perfectly miserable night and a perfectly miserable place over there to go with it all."

Certainly, 249 Hanover Street was not inviting. Although the brick pillars supporting the heavy gates, together with the wrought iron fence, would never keep out any determined intruder, they said "You Are Not Welcome" in a most effective way. If the message failed here, at the edge of the property, then the double doors under the dimly lit portico at the house itself took a second stab at it, for their design repeated the warning that visitors to 249 Hanover Street would not be pleasantly received.

Janet groaned as she forced herself out of the car into the pouring rain. She drew her heavy rain cloak tight around her shoulders and stared at the big house for a few seconds before walking back to an empty squad car parked at the curb behind her. She leaned in and switched off the flashing red lights, then made a note of the car's number before turning to walk quickly through the open gates. Staff Sergeant Janet Dexel hated fuss. She especially disliked police operations that attracted attention unnecessarily. Someone in her unit was going to get a dressing down as soon as she had the opportunity, and at the moment, the odds favored tonight.

Rain began to fall even harder so she broke into a run for the last few steps up to the double doors. Once inside, the sight of Chesley Barron-Ripple, or rather, what had been Chesley Barron-Ripple, quickly took her mind off the bad weather and the fool who had left the lights flashing. Two of her officers stood over the body. Neither was enjoying the assignment very much. One of them held a handkerchief over her nose.

Chesley Barron-Ripple was attracting the kind of attention that would have embarrassed him beyond measure had he been alive. An assistant from the medical examiner's office was snapping picture after picture of him where he lay on a priceless, silk-on-silk hand-woven rug. Behind the police officers, a pair of ambulance attendants, looking far more at ease than anyone else at the scene, were holding a body bag like a pair of Boy Scouts about to fold the flag at the end of the ceremony.

One of the policemen, the younger one, almost stood at attention as he addressed his boss. "The lab people have all gone, Sergeant," he said. "Except for him." The policeman nodded at the photographer. "And he's almost finished – *Aren't you?*"

It was clear to Janet that everyone wanted to get this part of the investigation over and done with.

"We're waiting for you to give us the clear." It was the other officer. She was speaking through her handkerchief. "Detective Andrew is in the next room with the three ... uh ... I guess they're suspects, aren't they?"

"Oh? Suspects?" Another thing that bothered Janet was having her officers jump to conclusions. Especially if there were media people nearby. One positive outcome of the heavy rain, however, was that the situation was free of the press, at least so far.

"Well, I mean ... I don't know if they're suspects. They're ... they're ... they've been *detained* by Detective Andrew."

The officer appeared relieved that she'd found the right word.

"There are three people," she continued with more confidence now. "There's the part-time handyman. And Barron-Ripple's daughter, and ... and ..." Her discomfort had returned. "And the *butler*, Sergeant Dexel."

Before Janet could reply, the younger policeman spoke again. "He said he was the butler, Sergeant, but I think he's really a kind of valet or personal servant. Anyway, he's got an alibi. He went to his sister's in Kennebunkport on the 30th. Been there for two days. Actually, all three have got alibis like that."

"I see," Janet Dexel said, searching her coat pockets for a tissue to pat the droplet of rain on her eyelash.

"Yeah, the daughter, Sergeant Dexel," the policewoman was still talking through her handkerchief. "She's ... well ... her alibi's pretty solid. She's been drying out in a clinic for the past month. Got back this morning. When she got home here she saw the butler ... uh ... valet, I guess, standing on the portico. Seems neither of them had a key so they sent for the handyman. He lives over in Lower Sackville."

"And what's *his* cover?" Janet wanted to know.

"Sounds reasonable enough," was the answer. "He comes once a week unless there's something special to do. Tomorrow's his day, and he missed last week. Says his wife and two neighbors can back it up."

"I see." Janet nodded at the body and then at the two ambulance attendants who still held the body bag stretched out. "I guess you can move him out of here now." To the police officers she said, "You two tell Andrew to advise that butler or valet or whatever he calls himself of his rights and then bring him downtown. I'll meet him there. Shouldn't be too hard to break up his story. You were right about 'suspect.' Just don't say it. Leave that kind of talk for the lawyers."

 What is Janet Dexel's reason for suspecting the butler rather than the daughter or handyman?

Solution on page 181

Head-on in the Middle of the Road

Judge Elmer Grieb of the Superior Court sat on the edge of an old wooden chair in his private office, elbows on his knees, chin in his hands, staring at the brown medicine bottle on his desk. *Karlsrhue Pharmacy,* the label said. *Take two tablespoons as required. DO NOT EXCEED RECOMMENDED DOSAGE.*

Elmer had already exceeded the recommended dosage. Three times. He was deep in thought, and whenever His Honor pondered over a case, he invariably reached into the bottom right-hand drawer for the helpful brown bottle from Karlsrhue Pharmacy.

The stress of making decisions in civil law suits had taken its toll on Elmer over the years. By his own admission, his nerves just weren't what they used to be. But he had a very low opinion of tranquilizers, indeed anything that came in the form of a pill. And years of listening to the so-called expert testimony of psychiatrists had entirely wiped away any faith he might have had in their powers. So, every morning of a day when he was about to endure the stress of handing down a decision, Judge Elmer Grieb turned to his own, oft-proven therapy. He filled a brown medicine bottle with home-made wine. Dandelion wine. His mother had taught him how to make it. According to Elmer's theory, the powerful amber liquid not only calmed his nerves and cleared his head, it was even a cure for his troublesome arthritis. And if the truth were known, it probably explained why he suffered far fewer colds than the rest of the population! Still another plus was that the stuff actually looked like medicine and tasted even worse, useful qualities in case any of the court staff got curious.

Earlier this afternoon, for two long and uncomfortable hours, Elmer had been formally and officially perched on the Superior Court bench feeling very much in need of his medicine. Over this time he had listened to the testimony of four witnesses: the two plaintiffs, the defendant appearing on behalf of Carrick Township, and the driver of the Carrick Township road grader. The case was one of those percentage-of-blame lawsuits that always made His Honor uncomfortable because he did not like to play Solomon.

It was a car accident case. Both plaintiff and defendant admitted to some blame. At issue was what percentage for each. Cases like these sometimes took Elmer a whole bottle of medicine to think through.

Several months ago, the two plaintiffs, traveling in separate cars at midday with no other traffic nearby, had run head-on into each other at the crest of a hill out on the Tenth Side Road of Carrick Township. At the scene of the accident the police had decided that since both drivers were smack in the middle of the road when they hit, they were mutually at fault. Hence no traffic charges were laid, and neither driver had been able to attack the other's insurance company. However, the two had now joined forces and, together, were suing Carrick Township and the township road foreman, Peter Hesch, on the grounds that it was road repairs to the hill in the week before their crash that had made it necessary for both of them to drive in the center. The two wore neck braces, and both produced medical certificates attesting to whiplash and other possible, as yet unknown, damage. They had managed to look seriously injured in the witness box.

When it was his turn to testify, Peter Hesch, the road foreman, acknowledged that yes, there had been road repairs on both sides of the hill the week before. It was a steep hill, he explained, and usually after a wet spring the hill was pretty rutted and full of potholes. It was a repair that the township carried out just about every year during a spell of nice, dry weather, he said. But then Peter Hesch managed to get the plaintiffs' lawyer all stirred up when he added, somewhat gratuitously, at the end of his testimony, that the two drivers had to be pretty stupid because "any damn fool should know you slow down and pull over when you get to the top of a blind hill."

At the reference to "blind hill" the plaintiffs' lawyer had practically danced with glee and took almost an hour of court time establishing that on this particular hill on the Tenth Side Road, it was impossible for a driver on either side to see a car on the other, until he reached the very top.

The fourth witness was Harvey Speelmacher, driver of the township road grader. To Elmer's considerable relief, Harvey's time in the witness box was brief and uneventful. Testifying in a case three years ago, Harvey had got very excited, and Elmer had had to adjourn for twenty minutes while the cleaning staff scrubbed wads of tobacco juice off the sides of the witness box.

This time it took Harvey barely a few minutes, a calm few minutes, to say that three days before the accident in question he had spent the morning with the township grader smoothing out the surface on both sides of the hill, the last step in the road repair. Then for no apparent reason at all, he added that he knew right well what day he had done it because it was his wife's birthday, August 9. He had booked off during the afternoon so he could take her fishing over on the South Saugeen, "bein' the weather'd been so nice and all."

After Harvey's testimony, the lawyers for both sides had summarized with surprising quickness, the plaintiffs' counsel arguing strongly that because the hill was a "blind hill," Peter Hesch and Carrick Township were at least eighty percent responsible if not one-hundred percent.

The gist of the argument from the defendant's counsel was that it was the two plaintiffs who were eighty percent responsible for what they had done to themselves, since common sense and safe driving obliged them to slow down and keep to the right in a situation where it might be a bit difficult to know what was coming from the opposite direction.

Elmer had recessed after that and directed everyone to return in one hour, at which time he would hand down his decision. That was eight tablespoons ago, and although he wasn't bothered by his arthritis anymore, he still had to go back into court and give his decision.

He reached for the bottle and the spoon one more time. This was definitely a ten-tablespoon case. What bothered Judge Elmer Grieb so much was the failure of the township side, the defendant, to bring up the most obvious counterpoint to the "blind hill" argument. And quite frankly, he didn't know what to do about it.

?

What is the important point that the township side has failed to bring up?

Solution on page 181

9

A 911 Call from Whitby Towers

Bev Ashby was so distracted by the size of the crowd gathered on the sidewalk that at first she didn't hear the doorman shouting at her.

"They're up there!" He was bent over the driver's door, yelling red-faced at the closed window and gesticulating wildly at the building across the sidewalk. "Fourth floor! But you have to walk 'cause the elevator's been down since yesterday!"

It wasn't until several hours later that Bev ruefully acknowledged, yet again, that maybe it's true what they say about cops: they just stick out. For the life of her she had no idea how the doorman had identified her, first as a police officer, and second, as the detective sent to investigate the incident. She was dressed in civvies, the car was unmarked, and she had used neither siren nor light. And there were several other cars at the curb that were clearly sent there by a police dispatcher. Yet the doorman had run out the revolving doors of Whitby Towers directly to her.

"Your uniformed people are up there! Two of them!" Bev had her window rolled down, but now he was yelling even louder. "And the chauffeur that saw him do it!"

His shouting increased the size of the crowd and drew their attention away from the incident that had been entertaining them in the middle of the busy downtown street. A noontime fender bender had developed into a slugfest between the two drivers involved. Both were now draped over the hoods of their respective cars in handcuffs.

Bev had to push the doorman back to get out of the car. He was still waving his arms and sputtering.

"I'm the one that called 911," he said into her face. "The chauffeur saw him doing it from down here on the street! Hanging himself. Yelled at me to call and then ran for the stairs!" The young man wasn't shouting anymore, but he was still wound up enough to draw even more of the crowd toward them. Bev took him by the arm and forced her way through the gawkers toward the doors of Whitby Towers.

"Shouldn't this be *your* job?" she said over her shoulder. "I mean, you're the one supposed to be breaking trail, aren't you?"

"Yes, omigod! Look, I'm sorry! This is only my second day. And I ... like ... I've never called 911 before! And I ..."

Bev pushed through to the revolving doors with the doorman in tow. Once inside, the plush quietness of the lobby calmed him with dramatic suddenness.

"Fourth floor," the doorman said with professional detachment. "Number 411. The stairs are over there behind that pillar. We're very sorry about the elevator problem."

Bev nodded. "I'll be back down in a while to talk to you. Just don't leave, please."

By the time she reached the fourth floor she was puffing a bit. She wondered how the occupants of Whitby Towers were tolerating a two-day elevator failure. It was an expensive building and even though "Towers" was an enormously pretentious title – the place had only six floors – a lot of money was needed for the rent here.

Suite 411 was easy enough to find, for a uniformed officer was standing in the hallway outside the door. He tipped his cap with his index finger as Bev approached. "Body's inside, Lieutenant. We have not cut him down; we've only been here," he looked at his watch, "seventeen minutes now. Chauffeur's in there with my partner."

He held the door open for Bev so she could see the entire tableau before taking a step. Suite 411 was a luxuriously appointed studio apartment. What marred the sight of the deep pile rug and highly polished reproduction furniture was the body of a silver-haired man, in excellent trim, hanging from a thin nylon rope, an overturned chair at his lifeless feet.

"His name is ..." The patrolman started to speak, but Bev cut him off with a shake of her head. Twice she walked slowly around the body and then expanded the circle to walk around the room. Everything was in perfect order, as one would expect at Whitby Towers. Well, not quite everything. The telephone wire was cut. Actually, not cut. Torn. That had taken strength. There was something else, too. Bev bent over in front of the balcony doors. What was it on the floor there, one end of a shoelace? No. Nylon rope. Looked like the same stuff that was around the dead man's neck. With a pen, she spread the drapes just enough to follow the rope to about knee level where the other end was clamped between the doors.

Nodding to herself, Bev looked up at the uniformed officer. "Now you can tell me his name," she said to him. "On second thought," she turned to the chauffeur, "you go first. Let's start with your name."

"Sandford Verity." No hesitation. He responded as though he'd anticipated her question. And he didn't talk the way Bev thought a chauffeur might, but then, she had to admit, she didn't really know any chauffeurs. Maybe they all talk this way! "What happened is very simple." He continued as though he were in charge. "My firm is Brock Livery Service. We pick up Mr. Seneca every day – that's his name, Audley Seneca – at 11:50 and take him to wherever he directs. It's a standing, daily order. Yesterday and today I came up here to his suite, because of the elevator situation, instead of meeting him in the lobby. You see, he has a prosthesis, an artificial leg actually, and the stairs are somewhat of a problem for him. This morning when I arrived I happened to look up. Thought maybe he might be watching that altercation on the street. That's when I saw him on the chair there, the rope around his neck. Of course I ran as fast as I could. Told the doorman to call 911. But I got here too late. The door was locked. What I should have done, I realize now, was get the doorman to come with me. With a master key. But then, after a crisis is over, one always thinks of things one should have done."

"Agreed, Mr. Verity," Bev said and turned to the uniformed officer. "Would you go down to the lobby," she said, "and bring the doorman up here? There's quite a big hole here in the story of Mr. Seneca's alleged suicide."

? **What is the "big hole" to which Bev Ashby refers?**

Solution on page 181

10

The Case of the Kramer Collection

George Fewster would never have admitted it to anyone, but had he learned how to use a modem and a fax machine when they first came on the market, he'd have taken early retirement even earlier.

It wasn't really early retirement in his case, as he was quick to explain to anyone who raised an eyebrow. It was more a second career. Instead of Professor of Archaeology at Simon Fraser University, he was now George Fewster, Consultant in Archaeology. The change in job description may have introduced a tad of uncertainty into his cash flow, but that was more than compensated for by what he had done this morning, as he did each morning. That was to walk past his car, where it sat silently in the garage, pause to marvel at the birds squabbling busily around the feeder, and then go into the little office he'd built for himself some distance from the house. There, perched on the lip of a small mountain meadow with the town of Banff to his left, Mount Rundle to his right, and the Bow River down below, he could be warmed by some of the most beautiful scenery in the world. Or, especially in autumn after the leaves had fallen, he could peer around a corner of his house and feel sorry for the commuters heading out to the city. He could even work, if he was disposed to – and he was, most of the time.

This morning for example. During the night, his modem had brought in a report from the Museum of Civilization in Gatineau that he'd been awaiting for over a month. When he got his computer going and brought up the *KRAMER* file, he was rewarded with a screenful of information.

The top of the screen read: *Contents of Kramer Estate Collection*. A short personal note followed:

Dear George,

You're going to have fun with this one. It's a weird conglomeration all right. Some of it is just collectibles, hardly even rummage-sale quality. But every once in a while, as you'll see, there's a real gem. There's also some very interesting Arctic exploration stuff, if it's genuine. And quite a few coins. I think these might be very valuable. Anyway, have fun.

Sincerely,
Myrna.

The *Kramer Estate Collection* had been offered to the museum – for a price – some six months ago by a couple from a small town in the Eastern Townships of Quebec. George had the name written down somewhere. So far, the museum had been able to establish that the collection was put together quite a few years before by one Francis Kramer, a successful but extremely eccentric prospector whose final years had been spent in the Thirty Thousand Islands area of Georgian Bay, where he'd held a running battle with the local bylaw and health authorities because he insisted on living in a dry cistern.

But the Museum of Civilization didn't really care about Kramer's lifestyle; it wanted an evaluation of his collection, and that is what George now turned to on his monitor.

Under the personal note from Myrna, the screen read *Group One*, then it gave more information that went like this:

These items in Group One, George, will not appear to need your attention at first glance. They are mostly old magazines, some of them are nicely dated though. There's a Reader's Digest *from 1922 and an 1890 edition of the* London Times. *A really exciting piece is a 1728 issue of the* Saturday Evening Post. *A genuine fraud, so to speak!*

George pressed PAGE DOWN on his keyboard. He wanted to get to the coins, but something in Group Two caught his attention. Group Two was a list of material that Myrna had called "Arctic exploration stuff." Most of it described artifacts from expeditions to the Arctic: items like the compass used by Robert Peary in 1906, Otto Sverdrup's toiletry kit, and a can of brown beans retrieved from a cache set up by the Rae expedition in 1854. What twigged George, however, was the description of a tract. *On the Origins of the Blond Eskimo,* the title read. *By Vilhjalmur Stefansson.* George made a note to have that one couriered to him right away and then kept pressing PAGE DOWN until the screen finally showed *Group Three: Coins.* This is what he wanted to see above all. There was another note from Myrna:

Can't wait till you come to Ottawa to see these face-to-face. This is where the real value is, I think.
There are two Washington half-dollars, 1792, in mint condition. Wait till you see them! And an Upper Canada half-penny from 1883 that looks so good you'd swear it was never in circulation. There are several of this type. But probably the most valuable are the three really old coins in the collection. From some time B.C.

There's a silver stater from Syria. It's fifth century B.C. The British Museum paid $4,000 for one of these last year and this one's in better condition, I'm told. The other two are Roman coins. They're both silver, too. One's from early in the reign of Caesar Augustus. Stamped 22 B.C., but unfortunately the profile of Augustus is not very good. The other one is about two hundred years later; you can't see the date, but the profile of Emperor Hadrian is as good as a contemporary issue! There's more in the collection. A whole bunch of beaver nickels from the thirties with George VI on them, and some of those funny blackout nickels from World War II, but they're probably not of much interest to the museum.

George leaned back in his chair and stared at the screen for a few seconds. Then, impulsively, he turned the computer off without even getting out of the file. He was disappointed.

Before this report had come in, he had looked forward to a trip to Ottawa, even if it meant he would have to join the commuters on a drive to the city. Now he knew the trip would likely be unnecessary.

?

What is wrong in the Kramer Collection that has left George Fewster so disappointed?

Solution on page 182

11

Waiting Out the Rain

Michelle Link sat in one of the two window booths at Kline's Soda Shoppe with Julie Varughese and two of their classmates from Memorial Junior School. All four stared gloomily at the rain pelting down on the street outside. They had headed straight for Kline's right after school, beating the crowd so they could get their favorite booth. It was a perfect location. In the corner at the window, the booth gave them a sweeping view of everybody in the little restaurant – more important, they could see who came in *with* whom and not be too obvious about it. As well, if the patrons failed to stir up any interest, they could usually find something diverting out on the street.

Not today, though. Except for two older ladies who had come in for tea, Kline's was unusually empty. So was the street. The rain had begun to fall the instant they arrived, hard enough to discourage any of the regulars from Memorial Junior and, except for two pedestrians who had taken shelter in the doorway of Vex's Pharmacy across the way, hard enough to pretty much empty the street, too. Now, two Cherry Cokes apiece later, and having exhausted the day's school stories, the four friends were bored and quite ready to leave, but the rain was not yet prepared to let them.

The only distraction, and the only person who seemed to be enjoying the weather, was a little boy standing in the gutter just off the sidewalk a few feet away from Michelle. He couldn't be more than three, Michelle calculated, watching him stand there in the water that sluiced down the gutter around his bright blue rubber boots, splashing up against and almost over the toes where someone – an older sister, Michelle speculated – had painted a large "L" on top of one and an "R" on the other with pink fingernail polish.

Through Kline's screened door, Michelle could hear the boy's squeal of delight as a candy-bar wrapper floated up to the toes, then made a complete circle and carried on between the boots. She followed the progress of the wrapper for a few feet and for the first time noticed the woman on the edge of the sidewalk. Must be the kid's mother, her speculation continued.

The woman was not watching her son – if it really was her son. She was standing under the awning at Whippany Appliances next door, listening transfixed to the radio bulletin booming from the store. Whippany Appliances was advertising Motorola, their new franchise brand, and a big cabinet model standing just inside the door put the news out onto the street.

Michelle could hear it from the restaurant:

"... from General Eisenhower's headquarters in England a confirmation that five divisions are involved: two American, two British, one Canadian. Early reports indicate that German troops have fallen back from the beaches at all five landing areas. Pockets of resistance are still strong, however, at Omaha Beach.

"The Columbia Broadcasting System's news service has also learned that ..."

For the past two days the radio news had talked of nothing but the landings at Normandy, the biggest invasion, it was being described, in the history of warfare. Michelle watched the woman stare vaguely into the appliance store. She had not once turned around to look at her little boy. He had his rain hat off now and was filling it with water.

"Michelle! Earth to Michelle! Hey, get with it! The rain has stopped! Remember? The wet stuff? Let's go while we can!" Julie finally reached across the table and shook her friend's arm.

"I wonder if her husband's a soldier?" Michelle said, without looking at Julie. "The little boy's father. I'll bet he is."

"What *are* you talking about?" Julie shook Michelle's arm one more time. "C'mon! The rain's let up. We've got to leave now or we'll have to order another Cherry Coke. Either that or rent the booth."

Michelle and Julie said goodbye to their friends at the doorway to Kline's and headed up the street. For a few seconds, they, too, paused at Whippany Appliances and listened to the radio talk about Normandy. The woman and the little boy were gone. Somehow they had disappeared as the girls were getting out of the booth. The street began to fill with activity again, almost as if it had been waiting, pent up and hidden under shelter until the weather improved.

The two pedestrians from Vex's Pharmacy had crossed the street and were moving on ahead of the girls. Farther up they could see Mister Lum at Lum's Groceteria pushing carts of fruit and vegetables back onto the sidewalk. Next to the appliance store two men got out of a truck belonging to Bitnik's Delivery Service and began to wrestle a soaking wet tarpaulin off a stack of cardboard boxes. Cars began to move up the street more quickly now, as though relieved by the prospect of drier progress.

Two minutes later, at the corner of Vine Street, Julie said goodbye, peeling off down Vine, leaving Michelle to continue on two more blocks to her home on Sanders Avenue. Michelle didn't expect to speak to Julie again until school the next day. For one thing, there was too much homework. More important, her parents had made one of those suggestions that parents tend to make about too much use of the phone on school nights.

The telephone rang anyway, about an hour after dinner, and it was Julie.

"Did you *hear* what happened? At Kline's?"

Michelle wanted to point out that obviously she had not, or why would Julie be calling, but she didn't get a chance.

"There was an accident! You know that truck? Bitnik's truck?" Julie was very wound up.

"It was right there when we passed. Remember? Those two guys unloading ... uh ... whatever it was? Anyway, *it rolled right into Kline's!* Right through the *window!* My dad says the brakes, no, no, the *emergency* brake probably failed."

"Julie ..."

"I mean, right where we were sitting!"

"Julie ..."

"Can you imagine? Like ... if it hadn't stopped raining? We'd have been sitting right there! We could have been killed! Or really injured or something!"

"Not just us, Julie. But listen ..."

"Don't tell your parents we were sitting right there in the window booth. I mean, I didn't tell *my* parents. You know what it's like. They'll get all worried and then they'll start thinking Kline's is dangerous and then ... well ... anyway. You know what parents are like. But isn't it *exciting?*"

"Julie!"

There was a pause followed by a soft and very tentative "What?"
"Julie, that was no accident."

?

Why is Michelle Link sure that what Julie Varughese has described was not an accident?

Solution on page 183

12

A Routine Check in the Parking Lot

Local legend had it that Dinks got its name in the 1920s when it sported one of the first neon signs in the county and the "R" in "*DRINKS*" refused to work. It didn't take a great deal of entrepreneurial flash for the then owner to realize that this fortuitous ellipsis had far more appeal to the passing public than his own four-syllable name, so Dinks the bar became, and Dinks it remained.

The name held up through a number of metamorphoses as the bar changed from a jazz cocktail lounge with upscale pretensions in its early days, to a dance hall catering to the army base nearby, to a jukebox *cum* hamburger joint, to its present phase: a cocktail bar again. It had a live trio on weekends, deep, ruby-red decor, cheap drinks and a reputation that struggled hard to stay just this side of sleaze.

The other constant in the history of the place was trouble with the police. Over the decades, the local force had learned to factor in Dinks as a normal part of their planning and projections. Situated on the edge of town, Dinks was where locals came to howl. So there were fights. Lots of fights. Most were the cracked-head, broken-tooth variety typical of a confrontation between drunks, but occasionally the brawls were serious.

Dinks was held up, too, with tedious regularity, almost always by strangers passing through who never knew where the real cash was kept. In the fifties, the huge parking lot had served as a track for post-midnight drag races, and in the sixties, as a spot for civil-rights sit-ins. Not long after the Vietnam War, it became known as a drug-exchange campus.

However, until this morning, there had never been a murder at Dinks. But now, even that marker had finally been achieved. In typical Dinks style as well. There was not just one body, but two. As it was, had Ron Forrester not been a veteran of some considerable experience on the police force, he might easily have bought into the murderer's ploy, for the bodies had been set up to look like the victims of accidental death.

It had been cleverly done. Dinks, quite naturally, was a choice rendezvous for illicit affairs. The bar was big, it was dark, it was on the highway, nobody asked questions, and no one would ever, ever, dare to bring a camera into the place. Therefore, when Ron cruised into the parking lot at 4:55 a.m., he was not particularly surprised to note that the large sedan, backed into the far corner of the parking lot, under the protective branches of an old elm tree, was occupied. There were two people in the front seat. For all he knew, there could have been two in the back as well. Not likely though.

Out of habit and not a little curiosity, Ron drove slowly toward the car for a look, leaving his high beams on to warn the two he was coming. After all, it was really no concern of his what two consenting adults were doing in a car at 4:55 a.m., even in the parking lot at Dinks. He just wanted to make sure they were consenting and that the consent was mutual.

The veteran policeman's first suspicion that something was

wrong came when he saw no reaction to his high beams. Usually in situations like this, the guilty parties tried to hide, or at the very least, turned around out of curiosity or annoyance. Then as he got closer and saw both heads lolling on the back of the front seat, he knew immediately that something was seriously amiss.

Ron accelerated the last hundred feet, then stopped. In a hurry now, he got out, ran to the car and pulled open the driver's door. It was too late. Without even taking a pulse, Ron Forrester knew from experience that both bodies had been dead for some time. He left the door open and went back to the patrol car, moving it perpendicular to the sedan so that the headlights would shine directly into the front seat.

On the other side of the man behind the steering wheel, a woman lay against the back of the seat, turned to one side, with her knees drawn up. Her shoes were off and her blouse unbuttoned. Her right hand dangled into the garbage can that straddled the center hump, and two fingers of her left were hooked into the man's belt. Ron couldn't see her face; it was tilted downward.

He could see the man's face, however. He'd been trying to ignore it all along, for the man sat leaning against the seat, his head turned to the left, eyes wide and lifeless, staring right at Ron, the whites gleaming in the lights of the patrol car. The pupils were tiny dots and the irises a washed out blue. The man's mouth was open, his tongue sticking out through lips that formed a perfect "O" as though he'd died in mild surprise. Like his companion in death, his shoes were off and his shirt unbuttoned. One hand lay on the seat beside him, the other, for what reason Ron could not figure, was stuck through the steering wheel, dangling at the wrist.

Ron turned on his flashlight and shone it around the interior of the car, even though the act seemed redundant in view of the powerful headlights behind him. The motor was still running, and there was about a quarter tank of gas left. The heater was on, too, set to "medium" with the fan set to "low." The radio played softly, an all-night station that Ron didn't recognize. In the back seat lay both headrests, a box of tissues, and a blue purse. Probably the woman's, for it matched the blue shoes on the floor beside her lifeless feet.

The veteran policeman reached across the dead man's body with great care to turn off the motor, then stopped, hardly believing what he'd almost done. Fingerprints! On the keys! This wasn't a case of two lovers forgetting about the potential danger of carbon monoxide. This was murder!

Slowly, and with even more care than he had used when reaching in, Ron withdrew his arm. The action brought his arm against the dead man's cheek, and in the morning silence he could hear the stubble rasp against his uniform. It made him shiver.

He shivered again just outside the patrol car and blew in his hands to warm them, as much because of the shock of what he had just seen as from the December cold. He looked up at the sky. No sunrise for an hour or more yet, he calculated, but then for the two in the car, no sunrise ever again.

?

How does Ron Forrester know that at least one and probably both of the victims have been murdered?

Solution on page 183

13

An Answer for Kirby's Important New Client

"Here's that guy again! That Smythe-Boliver!" Mara Silverberg was excited enough by her discovery to be shouting. "Listen!" She held up one of the faxed pages and read:

"'Major-General G. Smythe-Boliver, Royal Fusilliers: born 1708, at Ross-on-Wye; died 1779, at Chipping Sodbury; battles of Fort William Henry, 1757; Fort Carillon, 1758; Plains of Abraham, 1759. Fluent French and Spanish; signing delegate, Treaty of Paris, 1763.'"

"Yes, but," the voice belonged to her sister Krista, "the diary here is written by a *Major* Gerard Smythe-Boliver."

"So?" Mara was sure of her ground. "That doesn't have to mean he was a major forever, does it? Besides, how many officers in one war could possibly be named *Smythe-Boliver?*"

"You're probably right," Krista acknowledged. "In a war he'd get promoted faster. And he's upper class, so that means he gets to be a general, too, I guess."

Kirby Silverberg had been waiting patiently and finally broke in. This was, after all, her show. "Read that diary passage one more time, Krista," she said. "Remember it's *Fitzwall* we're interested in. More so than this Smythe-Boliver character."

Krista responded by lifting a page slightly and pushing her glasses to the bridge of her nose. "'Tuesday, 21 October,'" she read aloud, then put the paper down. "See?" she said. "Just like all the others. No year given." She shrugged and picked up the paper again. "Anyway." She cleared her throat. "'Only two months since the beginning of hostilities and I have just lost my batman, Fitzwall.'"

"What's a batman again?" Mara wanted to know.

"Personal servant. Sort of a valet," Kirby said. "Officers all had one then."

Krista started again "'... just lost my batman, Fitzwall. Poor chap; exactly half my age. Cannonball took his leg just below the knee, and three fingers. Not likely he'll survive. His wife died last year. One child. A girl born when the wife was but fourteen and he only four years her senior! One finds it difficult to understand the lower classes.'"

Krista looked up at her sisters. "There's a bunch of blather next about the need for more trained troops, and a piece about the amount of drinking going on. Stuff like that. Most of the rest is about the problem of having to train another batman. Nice guy this Smythe-Boliver! No more about Fitzwall."

She turned to Kirby. "I've gone back twenty entries and ahead twenty. There's not one other mention of Fitzwall. You want me to keep going?"

Kirby put her elbow on the huge volume of case-law summaries she had been wading through to keep the pages from fanning out.

"Please?" she said, pointing to the stack of photocopies in front of Krista and then to the pile in front of Mara. "There's so little time. You have everything there that the Imperial War Museum was willing to send from their Seven Years War collection. Mom's got the stuff from Halifax and Dad's got the memoirs. The answer's got to be somewhere here in all this stuff, and I need it by eight o'clock tomorrow morning or I lose the commission. Worse, I could lose the first big client I've ever had."

Kirby was referring to the Boston law firm of Tory, Wigan, and Best. She had been hired by the firm to uncover the year of birth of one Simon Fitzwall, first born of Ethan Fitzwall who had come to Boston with his father from England via Halifax, some time before the American Revolution. What was crucial was whether Simon had been born before or after 1788, the year the state of Massachusetts signed the U.S. Constitution. The date was important in a dispute over public versus private ownership of some land in the Boston area.

In their own search, the lawyers had been able to follow a straight track backward in time for almost two hundred years. Then the string broke. They had all kinds of data: personal histories, memoirs, diaries, photocopies of eighteenth-century newspapers, but the writers of the material, as was fairly customary for the time, seemed to have either a cavalier disregard for dates or simply felt they were unnecessary. Kirby Silverberg, P.I., had been hired to complete the paper chase. She had been given less than twenty-four hours to do it and had turned to her family for help.

As her sisters dug back into the material from the Imperial War Museum, Kirby turned to her mother. "Anything from Halifax yet, Mom?"

"I've been waiting for my chance!" the girls' mother replied. She had been poring over documents from the provincial archives of Nova Scotia.

"Listen to this." She took up the huge magnifying glass she had been using to decipher the barely legible print and held it with both hands. "It's from the harbormaster's report. 'Ship arrivals for the week.'" She looked up. "I guess I don't need to say it doesn't tell us what week. Or month or year either. In any case. 'Ship arrivals for the week: the *Endurance* and the *Titan* out of Portsmouth.' There's a long list like that. Must have been a real busy place! But get this." She shifted in her chair and rotated the magnifying glass. "The *Earl of Shannon* out of Southampton. Now ..."

She flipped over several pages to one with the corner pulled down. "Here. 'Harbormaster's Report to the Governor General.' It says:

'To Your Excellency's attention: with regard to the loss of the *Earl of Shannon* in Halifax Harbor on Sunday last, this ship until five years ago was the *Arquemada* out of Madrid. She was ceded to His Majesty's Navy under terms of the Treaty of Paris, along with ...' Then there's a list of other ships and stuff like that."

"But Mom," Kirby tried to keep the exasperation out of her voice. "That doesn't ..."

"I'm not finished. Listen. The report goes on to list the passengers from the *Earl of Shannon* who require passage on to Boston and who now await His Excellency's pleasure – he must have had to give them clearance or something, or maybe it was his responsibility after the ship sank. Anyway. Guess who's on the list? Fitzwall, Ambrose Esq., and three children, Abigail, Rachel, and Ethan!" She looked up triumphantly, blinking to clear the fuzz left by the magnifying glass.

"*All right Mom!*" This time it was Kirby doing the shouting. "Now all we need is ... Dad's got Ambrose's personal history thing. That's got to have the rest of what we need. Where is he? Where's Dad?"

"He's asleep," Krista said. "You know what happens. Soon as you mention lawyers he either goes to the bathroom or falls asleep."

"Take it easy. I'm here!" A male voice came from the corner of the room. "What do you need to know about Ambrose Fitzwall? I've become an expert interpreter of his memoirs."

"Memoirs, Dad?" It was Mara. "There's only three pages."

"Not quite that simple," Laurie Silverberg replied. He got out of the big easy chair and joined his family at the table. "The man was self-taught. Had to be. It takes some figuring to get past his spelling. And the sentence structure!" Laurie shook his head. "Listen to this. 'This here is the story of my family after my first wife Etta died and I lost the leg and my fingers with the major and I married Solomon Lesham's second daughter Nattie what was already a widow with one child Rachel we had Ethan right away and come to America with my Abigail.' Now that's all one sentence. You should try ..."

"Keep going!"

"Yeah, don't stop now!"

Laurie peered over his glasses and smoothed the curling edges of the photocopies with deliberate care before beginning again.

"'Nattie she died of the flux I never married again. We come to America on the *Earl of Shannon* a wormy tub she sank off Halifax good riddance.'

"You should see – he spells that R-I-D-N-E-S."

"Dad, c'mon!"

"Yeah, don't tell us the spelling. What happened!"

"All right, all right, all right. Let's see. Okay, yeah, '... good riddance. Abigail she had a hard crossing young Ethan being only half the age of her when I lost the leg and Rachel only twice that but it don't rain forever four years later Abigail married and two years after comes a baby girl then three more all girls. Then Rachel she got married and Ethan too at the same age Abigail was and all had the first babies two years after. Simon the only boy though ...'"

"Chauvinist!" Mara was indignant.

"Why doesn't he tell the girls' names?" Krista asked her mother who, in turn, raised her eyebrows at her husband.

"He doesn't," Laurie acknowledged almost sheepishly.

At first, none of them noticed Kirby waving her arms.

"It doesn't matter! It doesn't matter! I don't care if he's a chauvinist pig, we've got the answer! We know when Simon was born!"

How has the Silverberg family found the answer for Kirby's client? In what year was Simon Fitzwall born?

Solution on page 184

14

Two Shots Were Fired

The young policeman at the gate stiffened when he recognized the senior officer getting out of the car that had just pulled up. Instinctively, a hand went to his throat where his tie hung loosely around an open top button. Inspector Vince Pogor was a stickler for proper dress no matter what the weather, and the young constable knew it was too late now to rebutton his collar.

"You look like that when the media was here?" Vince was also known for getting right to the point.

"No. No, sir!" The young man's face, already soaking from the heat of the sun, began sweating even harder.

Vince lifted his hands to his hips. The gesture reminded him that he himself wasn't in uniform at all, that in fact he was in a T-shirt and shorts – kind of ratty ones to boot.

"Okay. Okay." he said. "Just ... Look, you know the regulation. Tie on or tie off. Not that half-way stuff. Now. Where's the shooting site? That it up there?"

"Yes sir!" The officer was so relieved he absently brought out a none-too-clean handkerchief to wipe his face. "Just around the corner of the building there. You'll see the yellow tape."

For a second or two, Vince toyed with the idea of going back to division headquarters to change clothes. The incident with the constable's tie had made him self-conscious about his own dress. In the end he decided not to. The media had been and gone, especially the TV cameras. Besides – he looked at his watch – the incident was already six hours old.

Vince was calling it an incident, not a *crime*, for the time being anyway. The evidence so far pointed in that direction. It was an accidental shooting, but a dicey one because of the victim. The dead man, Big Dino, was well known to Vince, in fact to just about everyone on the police force, especially the anti-racket squad which Vince headed up. Big Dino had roots deep in organized crime. Until this morning. This morning Big Dino had gone down with two bullets in the middle of his chest just outside the rear entrance to Galahad Storage. He'd been shot from inside the building by a security guard.

"Ah ... sir?" It was the constable. He'd taken his tie off. "Up there? Around the corner? Sergeant King ... ah ... he's waiting for you."

Vince grunted, just a wee bit embarrassed, then began to walk toward the rear of the building. He was glad to stretch his legs for he'd had a long drive. Officially, Vince was on vacation. The first two weeks of August were always his. That morning before anyone else in the family was awake, he'd taken a giant plate of bacon and perogies out to the deck of his cottage, despite the threat of rain, and had just snapped on the portable to listen to *The World at Eight* when the telephone rang, summoning him away from his beloved Lake Muskoka.

He'd headed down to the city right away, but changing out of the shorts and T-shirt did not even cross his mind. The heat wave that stretched from the American Midwest right up to the Arctic was so fierce that even the thought of full-length trousers made him sweat. And the heat was getting worse, too. On his way south, the dull sky that had covered most of eastern North America that morning reneged on its promise of rain and cooler weather, completely contradicting the weather forecasters. By the time Vince could see Toronto in the distance, the sky had turned blue and cloudless and the day was flatiron hot.

Not a day to spend walking on confounded asphalt, he thought, turning the corner where yellow boundary tape squared off a section of empty lot. He hardly noticed the tape at first, or even how much hotter it was on this side of the building. What caught his attention instead was the overwhelming, relentless noise from the traffic on the Queen Elizabeth Way. Ten lanes of speeding, bumper-to-bumper racket so loud he didn't hear Jack King until the third yell.

"Vinny! Vince! In here! Outa the sun!"

Vince ducked under the tape, stepped carefully over the chalk outline of a body, and walked through the only open door. It had a small sign that read "EMPLOYEES ONLY." Jack King was standing inside. His tie was pulled down and he had two buttons undone. Jack began to speak immediately.

"It was like this," he said. Vince realized that Jack had been waiting in the heat for some time and had no intention of dawdling through his report. He wanted to get back to headquarters and air conditioning.

"The guard sat here, his back to the door you just came through." He pointed to a battered metal chair and an old wooden table with a deck of greasy playing cards on top. "Says he was watching the front. That makes sense 'cause that's where all the break-ins have been coming through. Especially the one two days ago where one a' the other guards got beat up so bad."

Vince raised his eyebrows but said nothing. Jack went on. "Then all of a sudden, he says there's this dark shadow over him. From behind. From the doorway. He whips around. The sun's in his face.

There's an awful big guy there so ... *Boom! Boom!* Two in the chest."

"Sounds a bit trigger happy, don't you think?" Vince spoke for the first time.

"Yeah. But don't forget the guy was scared," Jack answered. "I mean, there's been so much trouble here. All the break-ins. They had that fire where the guy was trapped in a room. Then there's that guard who was beat up. Word is he'll never walk again. Can't say I really blame the guard for shooting. And Dino. He's a big guy. 'Sides, he had no business back here. We think he's a renter here. Least he had a key in his pocket. We're checkin' that right now. Anyway, how's the guard supposed to know? As it is, the place doesn't open to customers till nine o'clock. And not through this door." Jack was pointing out the door to the east. Through the opening Vince could see the skyline of the city in the distance and the surface of Lake Ontario shimmering in the brightness of midday.

"I don't know, Jack," he said. "It's still too neat. This door was open then?"

"Propped open," Jack answered. "Just like it is now. Haven't you noticed how hot it is in here? I can believe the guard when he says the door had to be open. And that means he couldn't hear anything either. With the highway traffic at that time of the morning."

Vince nodded. "Yeah, I guess so. Sounds like accidental shooting all right. There's only one thing that's not right."

"Yeah? What's that?" Jack King wanted to know.

? **What is the flaw in the security guard's story that Vince Pogor is referring to?**

Solution on page 185

15

Northern Farms Ltd. Versus Dominion Spraying Company

TRANSCRIPT: Docket #432

Court is now in session, the Honorable Mary-Joan Westlake presiding. First case is Docket Number 432: Northern Farms Limited, plaintiff, versus Dominion Spraying Company, respondent.

WESTLAKE: Thank you bailiff. Who is acting for the plaintiff?

DOYLE: I am, Your Honor. Douglas Doyle.

WESTLAKE: Ah yes, Mr. Doyle. We've met before. The Palgrave Poker case wasn't it? Well, never mind that. Would you summarize your claim, please?

DOYLE: Thank you, Your Honor. My client owns a farm bordering on the Bolton Canal and Regional Road 7. On the morning of 27 June last year, Dominion Spraying Company conducted an aerial spraying, in error, of a field in that farm. There were fifteen registered Holstein dairy cows in the field, nine of which subsequently died of the effects of the spray. My client is claiming damages of $147,000, plus costs.

WESTLAKE: I have your statement of claim here, Counselor. You have one of the dead animals valued at $122,000?

DOYLE: Yes, Your Honor; that's Molly's Arch Dream III. I will be introducing evidence showing that figure as representative of an offer made for her on 16 May last year.

WESTLAKE: All right, Mr. Doyle. Mr. T.A. Jones, you're appearing for the respondent?

JONES: Indeed, Your Honor. In the interest of saving time, may I state that Dominion Spraying Company acknowledges that spraying took place over the field in question instead of over Bolton Canal on June 27, and that some cattle in the field died subsequent to that event. My client does not acknowledge that the deaths of the animals are connected in a direct way to the effects of the spraying. For the record, my client has offered Northern Farms damages of $25,000 for inconvenience. The offer has been declined.

WESTLAKE: Unless my mathematics is suspect, $25,000 is precisely the amount of the total claim, less the value of – what's her name – Molly's Arch Dream III?

JONES: That's correct, Your Honor.

WESTLAKE: Very well. Okay, is the plaintiff ready to proceed?

DOYLE: Yes. Plaintiff calls Mr. Fenton Purge.

(Purge sworn.)

Mr. Purge, you are the manager of Northern Farms Limited?

PURGE: That's right. We have a total of seven operating farms specializing in Holstein cattle and Landrace swine.

DOYLE: The property where the spraying took place on 27 June: would you describe it for the court?

PURGE: It's … well, a one-hundred-acre parcel bordered by a conservation area on two sides and by Bolton Canal and Regional Road 7 on the other two. We refer to it as Farm Number 3.

DOYLE: Specifically, I meant the field that was sprayed.

PURGE: Oh. Well, that's a ... a ... well, a square field about twenty-five acres in the southwest corner of the farm. It's about ...

WESTLAKE: Mr. Doyle, what's this for? The respondent isn't denying that the spraying took place. Or where.

DOYLE: Background, Your Honor; I'll be brief. Mr. Purge, tell us what happened at this field on the morning of 27 June.

JONES: Your Honor, it hasn't been established that this witness was present at the field on the morning of June 27!

WESTLAKE: Mr. Doyle?

DOYLE: Very well ... uh ... Mr. Purge, what happ ... rather, were you summoned to the, to Farm 3 on 27 June?

PURGE: Yes, in the early afternoon, when it was discovered that cattle were down in the field – collapsed. I moved fast 'cause that's where we'd pastured Molly's Arch.

DOYLE: Surely you called a veterinarian?

PURGE: Indeed. Dr. Logan confirmed the cause of the collapse as reaction to a chemical used in insect control.

JONES: Objection!

WESTLAKE: Oh, really? On what grounds, Mr. Jones?

JONES: I think the court would prefer to hear expert testimony from the expert, not secondhand.

DOYLE: We'll be calling Dr. Logan, Your Honor. No more questions.

WESTLAKE: Any cross, Mr. Jones?

JONES: Yes, thank you. Mr. Purge, is it customary to let an animal that is supposedly worth $122,000 wander around a pasture field?

PURGE: Entirely. Happens all the time when the rest of its herd is pastured. Cows are very social animals. It's not unusual for them to go into decline if they're isolated. You just need good fences, and we have that. Well, not from above though!

WESTLAKE: Confine yourself to the questions, Mr. Purge.

JONES: No more for this witness.

(No re-examination; plaintiff calls Eulalia Bean; sworn.)

DOYLE: Ms. Bean, you are an employee of Northern Farms Limited?

BEAN: Summer help. I'm a university student, but I work summers at the Canal Farm ... we call it Canal Farm.

DOYLE: And you were responsible for the care of the cattle in the field in question?

BEAN: I put them in there on June 21. Fifteen black and whites. Including Molly.

DOYLE: Molly's Arch Dream III?

BEAN: Yes. We call her Molly.

DOYLE: What do you normally do to care for the cattle?

BEAN: When they're pastured like that it's mostly supplement feeding and water checks. And of course you keep an eye on them.

DOYLE: Supplement feeding and water checks?

BEAN: Pasture's not good this year so I take hay out with the tractor twice a day. To a feeding trough. And there's no water in that field so we pipe it out from the barn. Water trough's right beside the feed trough at the fence. I always check that the float valve's working right.

DOYLE: And did you take out hay and do a water check on the morning of 27 June of last year?

BEAN: Yes, about 5:30. Sun was just coming up.

DOYLE: Did you check on Molly's Arch ... uh, Molly?

BEAN: That's even more automatic than checking the water!

DOYLE: And she was well and healthy?

BEAN: Standing orders are that if she's not, we call the vet, then the manager, in that order.

DOYLE: Thank you. That's all I have. Mr. Jones?

JONES: Ms. Bean. On the morning of June 27, did you actually see the airplane spray the field and the cattle?

BEAN: Actually, no. I was just turning back into the barn when I heard a plane in the distance, but there's nothing unusual about that. Besides, I had machinery running in the barn.

JONES: Well then, just when did you become aware that there might be a problem with the cattle in your care?

BEAN: When Mrs. Organ phoned about two o'clock to tell me.

JONES: That's all I have of this witness, Your Honor.

(No re-examination; plaintiff calls Parthenon Andreikos; sworn.)

DOYLE: Mr. Andreikos. Where were you at approximately 5:30 a.m. on 27 June of last year?

ANDREIKOS: In my truck on Road 7. Goin' south toward the canal to ... uh, you want me to say what I saw?

DOYLE: Go ahead.

ANDREIKOS: So. I waved at Eulie ... uh, Eulalia. Miss Bean. She'd just come out of the barn with the tractor. Then I drove past the herd. So. You want to know where I was going?

DOYLE: It won't be necessary. Are you familiar with a Holstein dairy cow called Molly's Arch Dream III?

ANDREIKOS: Oh sure.

DOYLE: And you saw her in the herd there?

ANDREIKOS: She's awfully hard to miss. Really big. And she has – well, *had* anyway – this most unusual mark on her right side. A perfect triangle. Takes up her whole side. Never saw anything like that, ever. Mostly on Holsteins, it's blotches.

DOYLE: For you to see that, the animal had to be broadside to you.

ANDREIKOS: So. They were lined up at the feed trough. You see, soon as they hear the tractor they know Eulie's coming and they get ready. Cows aren't as stupid as people think.

DOYLE: Molly's Arch Dream was at the end of the line then?

ANDREIKOS: Cattle always feed at the same spot. Same way they always go to the same stall in the barn. Every time. So. The end of the trough pointing to the road must have been her spot.

DOYLE: Mr. Jones?

JONES: Mr. Andreikos, are you usually driving around in your truck at 5:30 in the morning?

ANDREIKOS: In the summer. I'm in the feed business. My customers are up even before then. So.

JONES: I gather Northern Farms is a customer of yours.

ANDREIKOS: Oh, yes.

JONES: Seven farms. They must be quite a customer!

DOYLE: Objection! Your Honor, my friend here is very close to making allegations!

WESTLAKE: You know better, Mr. Jones!

JONES: No more questions.

(Plaintiff calls Daphne Organ; sworn.)

DOYLE: Mrs. Organ, you are a neighbor of Northern Farms Limited Number 3?

ORGAN: Right across the road. Born in that house. Lived there seventy-eight years now.

DOYLE: Where were you at approximately 5:30 a.m. on 27 June?

ORGAN: On my front porch. That's where I have my tea.

DOYLE: Could you tell the court what you saw that morning?

ORGAN: I saw young Eulie take hay to those cattle.

DOYLE: What else?

ORGAN: Then I saw her go back to the barn.

DOYLE: After that.

ORGAN: I saw the airplane come. It flew – it was almost touching the ground! Spraying this terrible-smelling stuff. All over the cattle, too! It's a disgrace!

DOYLE: You saw the spray hitting the cattle?

ORGAN: Of course! And all over the field, too.

DOYLE: Then what did you do?

ORGAN: I went inside. I told you, it smelled!

DOYLE: We have heard from other witnesses that it was you who first noticed the cattle in trouble, and that you then telephoned Ms. Bean. Is that right?

ORGAN: Don't know if I was first. I only know what I saw. Those poor cattle staggered like drunks! When two o' them fell I got on the phone.

DOYLE: What time was that?

ORGAN: After my lunch. I have my lunch on the porch at one o'clock. Nice and shady then on hot days.

DOYLE: Your witness.

JONES: Are you familiar with a dairy cow called Molly's ...

ORGAN: Of course I am. Who wouldn't know about a cow worth more than a hundred thousand dollars? Then she's got that funny triangle. Never heard of anything like that on a Holstein before.

JONES: Did you see this particular cow that morning?

ORGAN: I can't say for sure I saw her specifically. There's more to my life than watching cows, you know. I go out on my porch to have tea and watch the sunrise.

JONES: I understand. No more questions. Well, yes, one more. Mrs. Organ, didn't the terrible smell keep you from having your lunch on the porch?

ORGAN: The wind. Nice breeze blowing the other way. I wouldn't have gone out otherwise. I may be old but I'm not a fool, you know.

DOYLE: I have some re-examination, Your Honor. Mrs. Organ, could you pick out Molly's Arch Dream in a herd?

ORGAN: I already said I could.

DOYLE: Did you see her in the field from time to time prior to 27 June?

ORGAN: I surely did.

(Plaintiff calls Dr. Robert Logan; sworn.)

DOYLE: Would you describe your professional work, Dr. Logan?

LOGAN: I am a veterinarian in private practice.

DOYLE: Your Honor, I have here an autopsy report on the nine cattle in question, dated 28 June and signed by Dr. Logan. Mr. Jones has a copy. I would like to enter it as an exhibit.

WESTLAKE: Very well.

DOYLE: Dr. Logan, you describe the cause of death for the nine cattle as respiratory failure in reaction to a chemical substance. Does this apply to Molly's Arch Dream as well?

LOGAN: It does.

DOYLE: All yours.

JONES: Dr. Logan, would you explain the phenomenon "hardware disease" to the court?

WESTLAKE: Hardware disease? This better be relevant, Mr. Jones.

JONES: With respect, Your Honor, it's crucial to our response.

WESTLAKE: Very well. Let's hear about hardware disease then.

LOGAN: Indeed. Now, mammals of the suborder *Ruminantia*, which includes the *Typloda* ... uh, camels, and the *Pecoran:* deer, giraffe and so on, and of course the *Bovidae*, your cows – all these have multi-chambered stomachs. Now ...

WESTLAKE: Maybe a briefer approach is in order, Dr. Logan; I'm not sure we need a whole anatomy course.

LOGAN: Yes, I see. All right then. Now ... now ... a cow's stomach has four chambers. Most of what a cow eats is swallowed whole, goes to one of the chambers, comes back up again to be chewed as cud, and is reswallowed to another chamber. You see, when they graze they tend to scoop and tear, often picking up stones and bits of metal and garbage from the ground. It collects in one of the chambers. Usually stays there for life. Sometimes a beast will swallow something that just can't be stored and it can cause problems.

JONES: Are the symptoms obvious? Of hardware disease, I mean?

LOGAN: It's not all that common a thing. When it happens though, the problems can develop very fast.

JONES: Your autopsy report states that Molly's Arch Dream III had hardware disease at the time of her death. Is that right?

LOGAN: Yes, but that's not unusual. You notice in the report that several of the other cows had it, too.

JONES: But Molly's case was advanced.

LOGAN: It was serious.

JONES: Quite possibly fatal? In fairness, by the way, I should tell you that I will be calling an expert in animal anatomy to comment on your report.

LOGAN: It might have been fatal.

JONES: In fact, is it not possible that Molly's Arch Dream III was already dead when the airplane sprayed the field on June 27?

DOYLE: Objection! The witness has already testified as to the cause of the death!

WESTLAKE: I think I'd like to hear his answer, Mr. Doyle. It might clear up some of the fuzziness we've been listening to from previous witnesses.

?

What is the "fuzziness" Judge Mary-Joan Westlake is referring to?

Solution on page 185

16

An Unlikely Place to Die

Because of the traffic, mostly the snarl at the underpass on Wolfe Road, Brad Matchett got to the scene an hour later than he'd said he would. A late afternoon thunderstorm yesterday, with high winds and heavy rain, had caused so many power outages that some traffic lights were still out, making the morning rush hour worse than usual. Normally, Brad would have slapped the red flasher on the roof and driven around the line of cars, but because of the underpass, he couldn't do that. To make matters worse, he'd then made a wrong turn. The big estates in Cedar Springs were set in a maze of crescents and cul-de-sacs and one-way streets designed to discourage all but the most committed drivers. He'd become so lost he was forced to call the dispatcher to find out where he was.

The only upside in this case so far, it occurred to Brad, if indeed there can be upsides for the head of a homicide division, was that being late wasn't really a disaster because an accidental death, even if drugs are involved, is not usually a light-flashing, siren-blaring matter. Unless of course the victim happens to be a *somebody*.

In this case, it was close. The victim was almost a somebody. Not quite, but almost. Mme Marie-Claude de Bouvère appeared from time to time on the social pages of *The Enterprise*. Not so much because she was the wife of the former Haitian ambassador; more because she was a one-time tennis star. Good enough for two cracks at Wimbledon in her teens. That made her status too close to call, so Brad had gone out himself just to be on the safe side.

Mme de Bouvère had been discovered shortly after sunrise by her gardener. The body lay in a gazebo set between the de Bouvères' huge house and their tennis court. On a table in the gazebo, along with her tennis racket, were all the appropriate paraphernalia for preparing and injecting a substance. Her tennis bag held three small bags of white powder. Brad knew all this from Sergeant Willy Peeverdale who, until Brad managed to get there, was the investigating officer in charge. For now, that was the extent of his information because the underpass on Wolfe Road had cut off radio communication. Now, almost an hour later, Brad was finally turning into a circular drive that looped the huge property at 23 Serene Crescent.

The property was very private. So were all the estates in Cedar Springs. A screen of sycamores and magnolias lined Serene Crescent so that even the most intrepidly curious driver would never see the house. Just to be sure, another screen, Colorado blue spruce this time, duplicated the effort about fifty paces behind the other trees. Interesting, Brad noted. Not one cedar.

Had it not been for the yellow crime-scene tape on the south side of the house, he would have spent yet more time looking for the gazebo, but the tape led him through a grove of honey locust and along a path of brick chips to the back of the house. The property here was even larger than the front. The gazebo, big as it was – to Brad it looked more like the band shell in Misty Meadows Park – appeared almost lonely and curiously out of place. It sat precisely midway between the house and the tennis court, completely surrounded by a perfectly manicured lawn.

"Nothing's touched, but we gotta move fast 'cordin' to the coroner." The voice behind him made Brad jump. He would never get used to Peeverdale's habits. The sergeant made no small talk, ever. He never said "hello"; he never said "excuse me." And if he was aware that he made people nervous by suddenly appearing behind them, he'd never made any effort to change.

Peeverdale pressed on. "Says she can confirm the drug thing better the sooner she gets into the postmortem. Figures death occurred between ten and eleven last night. Sure looks like they OD'd. The guy died first she thinks, but only by a bit."

"The guy? They?" Brad realized he was sounding excited.

"Yeah." Peeverdale was never flapped either. "Guess that didn't come through on your radio. Y'see, the gardener, he saw Maa-daam de … de … whatever … lyin' there in that thing, that gay-zee-bo, and he split for the phone. Waited for us in the driveway. We found the guy. Figure it's Mister … Mon-soor de Boov … Boo … I can't get the doggone name right! Anyway we found him on the ground on the other side. Looks like he was sittin' on the rail and went over. For sure it's the missus on the floor, 'cordin' to the gardener. The guy's got no ID on him."

Sergeant Peeverdale dropped a pace behind Brad as they approached the gazebo, but continued talking. "Looks like the two of them were gonna play a little tennis last night. Or maybe they already played, it's hard to tell. And then they figured they'd get a little buzz on. My guess is they got some hot stuff they weren't expectin' and it did them in."

There were two steps up into the gazebo, and Brad stopped on the first one to study the body of Mme de Bouvère lying flat on the floor. Well, not really flat. Reclining was more like it. The woman appeared so composed, so much an elegant study in white. Not a mark or a smudge or a speck on the white blouse or the white tennis skirt or the white sneakers. Except for the slight pinch to her eyes, it looked as though she had known she would be seen like this and had prepared for it.

Peeverdale, meanwhile, had not interrupted his monologue. "Gardener found her there at about 7 a.m. Comes every other day to mow the lawn. S'pose that's why it looks like a billiard table. Mine sure don't look like this. Anyway, he came to get some equipment he left yesterday and noticed the lights on over the tennis court. That's when he saw Maa ... her. He didn't see the guy. You gotta look over the rail to see him. Uh ... the coroner, she wants us to hustle, Captain. It's the drug thing. Says the sooner the better."

"Tell you what, Peev," Brad said. "You give her a call. Tell her we'll be a while. We've got to figure out first where this lady died. And maybe the guy, too."

"You mean," Sergeant Peeverdale reached inside his tunic and scratched absently, "you don't think she died right here?"

"No," Brad replied. "I don't."

? **Why does Brad Matchett think that Mme de Bouvère did not die at the gazebo?**

Solution on page 187

17

To Catch a Mannerly Thief

As she stepped over the potholes in the street and leaned hard into a fierce east wind, Agnes Skeehan made a promise to herself: never again was she going to attend a conference in November unless it was within walking distance of the equator. Actually, for Agnes, anywhere warmer than Liverpool would do. Liverpool may have produced the Beatles, and it could point with pride at its importance to the Industrial Revolution, but to Agnes that was hardly enough to make up for the miserable weather.

She mounted the curb, trotted across the sidewalk, and pulled hard at the entrance door of her hotel. Three days at the Birkenhead Arms had taught Agnes to yank with both hands at the ancient portal.

"Ah, young missy!" It was the hotel porter. He made a contribution all his own to Agnes's opinion of Liverpool. "You've got a telephone message here, young missy. All the way from Canada! A Deputy Commissioner Mowat. Sounds important, missy. Talked to him myself, I did. Told him you were out, I did."

Agnes mumbled a thank you as she grabbed the message and ran for the creaky old elevator. As things stood at the moment, she was only three hours away from her flight home, but she had a feeling this call was going to change her schedule.

It did.

"I want you to stay over there in Liverpool and help them with this case." Deputy Commissioner Mowat's voice crackled and sputtered across the Atlantic only minutes later. "As a favor from us, you know, international police cooperation and all that." He paused, but then jumped in again as though to head off the objection he was expecting. "You're simply the best there is on handwriting. They don't have anybody that comes close to you. Now what I want you to do right away is go to their headquarters – it's right by your hotel there – and report to Superintendent Anthony Opilis. He's the head of their C.I.D: their Criminal Investigation Department. Now what I want you to do is consider yourself on temporary assignment there. Indefinite. As long as it takes."

Agnes struggled so hard to keep from telling Deputy Commissioner Mowat where he could stuff the international cooperation and the temporary assignment that she barely heard the rest. She didn't really need to though. The tabloids were full of the case that prompted his call. "The Friendly Filcher" one daily called it. "The Case of the Courteous Cat Burglar" another dubbed it. Whatever he – or she – deserved to be called, the case involved an amazingly successful thief who was breaking into homes and stealing jewelry. He seemed to have a peculiar respect for his victims, and this, in addition to the size of the take, was what the papers found so interesting. At each theft – there had been seven now – the thief left behind a neatly handwritten note of apology and an assurance that the stolen pieces would find their way only into the hands of people who would appreciate their beauty and value.

These notes, Agnes knew, were the reason she was being loaned to the Liverpool C.I.D. Mowat was right when he called her the best.

Agnes Skeehan, *Corporal* Agnes Skeehan, fourteen-year veteran of the Royal Canadian Mounted Police, had a special interest and an even more special knack in handwriting analysis. At graduation from the police training college in Regina, circumstances had presented her with a choice of more study, or assignment to a mounted patrol at the Parliament Buildings in Ottawa. Since race-track betting windows were as close to horses as Agnes ever cared to be, she picked the study and had never looked back. Eight months ago, her article in the *Journal of Forensic Science* had led to an invitation to address a conference in Liverpool. Little did she realize when she came down from the podium there, to a huge round of applause, that the next move would be, not to the airport, but into the superintendent's office at the Liverpool C.I.D.

Superintendent Opilis, a long-time acquaintance of Deputy Commissioner Mowat as it turned out, was a plodder. His explanation of the jewelry thefts to Agnes was so detailed and so slow that she had to fight to pay attention. She kept turning her head toward the grimy office window to yawn, covering the move with a phony cough.

The superintendent must have sensed her mood for suddenly Agnes became aware of annoyance in his voice.

"Withenshawe?" he said, or rather, asked. "I say, Corporal Skeehan. You heard me? Withenshawe Purveyors?"

Agnes blushed. She had indeed been drifting. The problem was, she just didn't want to be in Liverpool.

"Yes, Superintendent, I'm sorry." She got up and walked to the window, trying to appear alert by focusing on a weathervane pointing at her from atop a pub across the street.

"Withenshawe Purveyors of Speke Street." She cleared her throat. "Every one of the notes was written on Withenshawe's letterhead. I'm aware of that. And your people have definitely established that they were all written by the same left-handed person. I'm aware of that, too. But don't you think the Withenshawe Purveyors stationery is a most clumsy red herring? After all, who ..."

"Indeed, indeed Corporal Skeehan." Opilis got up and joined Agnes at the window. "But you see, there are other serious reasons why Alistair Withenshawe is a right handy suspect." He paused awkwardly. "We ... er ... we've summoned him. His office is just a short walk south of here. What we want you to do is ... Why! That's him! Right there. Across the street."

"Him?" Agnes pointed at a tall, very nattily dressed gentleman holding down a bowler hat. "The dude with the hat? And the cane? Look at him!" Agnes was fully awake now. "Does he always walk like that in public?"

"Yes, well," Superintendent Opilis was almost apologetic. "Ah, we have dealt with him before. I'm afraid he's a bit of a showman."

To prove the policeman's point, Alistair Withenshawe, who had been bouncing his cane off the edge of the curb and catching it, now began to twirl it high in the air like a drum major, spinning it first over one parked car, then the next, and then a third, before he brought it down and made a crisp military turn off the walk and into the street toward the police station.

Opilis let a touch of admiration creep into his voice. "Snappy, what?"

Agnes looked at him. "Yes, I agree. Snappy. But I'll give you any odds you want he didn't write those notes."

?

Why is Agnes Skeehan so sure of that?

Solution on page 187

18

Tracing the Couriers from Departure to Arrival

"Seamus? Did I get that right? *Seamus*?" Mary Clare McInerney realized she was shouting the instant she saw heads in the outer office turn in unison toward her. She didn't have a lot of choice, however. The connection was very poor.

"Is that a first name or a last name? A code name more likely. Which?" she wanted to know.

She waited for the unnerving pause so typical of transglobal telephone calls, particularly from places like Northern Africa, the delay that always made callers think they'd lost their call. But the answer came through. Struan Ritchie was at the other end of the conversation. He was in Addis Ababa and he was shouting even louder than Mary Clare.

"Yes, Seamus!" Struan's voice was buried in crackle and hiss. "It's the only name I have, so it's likely a code name. The other one I have is a single name, too: Rothsay."

"Rothsay!" This time Mary Clare really turned the heads in the outer office. To make it worse she had forgotten the transmission delay and had almost spoken over the rest of Struan's sentence. It was important information.

"... say," Struan was saying, "is the one who is flying out of Dorval in Montreal. It's confirmed. But I don't know where she's going."

Mary Clare waited and then, as quietly as she could in her excitement, said, "She?" and waited again.

"Yes, *she*," was the reply. "Two of the four couriers, it would seem, are women. Rothsay is one of them."

"And 'Saint' is the other then." Mary Clare didn't wait this time. "We got that yesterday. So that means 'Seamus,' and the other one we got yesterday, 'Felipe,' are males. Well, that helps. Not much though if they are good at disguises. What we really need to know is where each of the four is going and what airport they're flying out of. The only way we can coordinate this bust is if each of the couriers is tailed from departure to destination and nailed when they arrive. That way we scoop the parties at both ends, too."

Struan's voice came in over top of Mary Clare's. "I've got to get off. There's a lineup behind me and there's something going on down the street. Listen. I've got two more pieces. Seamus is going to Brazil, to Rio. Got that? But I don't know where he is now or what airport he's going to use. The other is ..."

At that point there was a fierce crackling on the line, followed by an electronic whirr, and finally a dial tone. This time, Mary Clare's shout of frustration brought the entire outer office to its feet. She chose the moment to wave Harvey Bottrell and Cecile King into her office.

Mary Clare McInerney was a member of the Drug Enforcement Administration working out of "E" Division in Seattle. For the past six months she had been coordinating a team investigation into an illegal narcotics ring. Over the last three days, things had come together at a rapid pace; the team was about to close in on the four key couriers and, through them, the leaders of the ring.

What her team had been able to put together was that each of the four couriers, within the next forty-eight hours (using GMT-9 as the reference point, because she was working out of Seattle), would be flying to separate destinations with major deliveries. Mary Clare was certain her team could break the ring if the four could be identified and followed from airport to airport. They now knew who the four were. At least their code names – that was enough.

"That was Struan Ritchie in Addis Ababa," she said to her two assistants after they had seated themselves at the coffee table in her office.

Harvey nodded. "We know."

"The whole office knows," Cecile added.

Mary Clare reddened slightly. "It was an incredibly dirty line," she explained, "with all kinds of ambient noise from where he was phoning, too. Sounded like he was out in the street. Come to think of it, he could even have been on an off-shore phone. The real problem is I think he had more to give us before the line broke down."

"Maybe what we've got will make you feel better," Harvey said. "Just some little pieces, but we're definitely getting closer."

Mary Clare got up from her desk and joined the two at the coffee table. "Lay it out," she said.

"We have three of the destinations," Harvey took three pens from his jacket pocket and set them on the table. "At the very least we can put a blanket surveillance on the airports." He held up both hands, palms out, before Mary Clare could say the obvious. "I know that's not what we want, but ... anyway, one of the couriers is going to Hong Kong. That information is just five minutes old. It came in while you were talking to Struan. Another is going to Hawaii, to Oahu."

Cecile leaned forward. "And one is going to Bermuda. Better than that, we also know this one will be flying out of Orly, in Paris, to get there." She leaned back again. "What we don't have is who any of them are. We only know that three couriers are going to these three places."

Mary Clare picked up one of Harvey's pens from the table and began to play with it, bending it with both hands into a bow shape. "What did you come up with in the call to Chicago?"

Harvey made a face. "According to our contact there, uh ... uh ... do you think I could have my pen back?"

Cecile finished for him. "One of the couriers is definitely leaving from O'Hare there. But we had the destination wrong before. Originally, we thought it was Hawaii, but it's not, and we don't know what it is, either."

Mary Clare was sufficiently distracted by this information for Harvey to surreptitiously retrieve his pens, all three, and stuff them back into the safety of his jacket pocket.

"So." Mary Clare was speaking to no one in particular. "So. We are this close." She made a tiny space with her thumb and forefinger. "If only the time wasn't so short. If ..."

"Mary Clare!" Cecile was pointing at the winking light on her desk. "Your telephone. Wonder if that's ..."

It was Struan Ritchie again.

"Sorry about that cutoff before." The line was very clear this time. "Just down the street, these two guys on a camel ... Why am I telling you this? You'd have to be here. Listen. This is what I didn't give you. You know that Felipe, the one you said you got yesterday?"

Mary Clare nodded as though he were sitting in the office.

"Well, I've had that one for a little while but couldn't confirm it. Guess if you got it from a different source, it must be right. Anyway, Felipe is at Heathrow right now, according to my information. In the departures lounge. Where he's going, I don't know. It's not Hong Kong, if that helps. Wish I could tell you, but I can't."

"No need." Mary Clare McInerney had a huge smile on her face.

"That's the last piece of the puzzle." She held back the receiver so her grin could include the two assistants. "Let's call out the dogs," she said, "the chase is on!"

?

How has Mary Clare McInerney figured out where each courier is going and where each is flying from?

Solution on page 188

Not All Lottery Winners Are Lucky

For at least the tenth time that day, Captain Frank Ricketts pulled his head down turtle-like into his coat and wondered how on earth his parents could possibly have left Jamaica for a climate like this.

He pulled his hat down, too, so it would fit tighter over his head. The business of headgear was another issue. Just inside the back door of his home there was an array of hats and caps of every possible weight and design, and never once did he seem to pick the right one as he left in the morning.

Chinooks. That's what everyone called the extreme, almost instant changes in weather here in Calgary. Abrupt rises in temperature of up to twenty degrees, sometimes in less than an hour. "It's what you get for building a city on the east side of the Rocky Mountains," everyone in Calgary said, as though the first pioneers had planned it that way. "You just have to get used to it," was always the next comment. Frank had never gotten used to it.

He took a step toward the body, trying to put chinooks out of his mind and being careful to put his feet down flat in the snow. He also had the wrong shoes on for these conditions and didn't want to slip and fall.

It had been a typical Calgary winter so far. Two days ago, right in the morning rush hour, a sudden chinook had turned the snow into slush. Then, before noon, the temperature had plunged to Arctic levels and stayed that way until earlier this morning when it warmed up just enough for snow to fall for an hour. Frank knew that one careless step on a layer of snow over ice would put him on his backside. That was an indignity he didn't need in front of the whole crime scene crew, so he was very cautious as he approached the body and squatted down beside it.

"His name is Archie Deschamps-Lebeau, Captain. Or was anyway." Frank looked up to see Nick Andropolous, the oldest member of the homicide unit. Nick secretly fascinated Frank, for even though he had been born and raised in Crete, he always dressed like a typical urban Canadian, with no hat, no gloves, boots undone and coat open.

"Seventy-three years old. Widower," Nick went on, reading from a ragged spiral-bound notebook pinched between his thumb and index finger. "Lived alone in the house over there. Stinking rich."

Nick closed the notebook and hunkered down across from Frank. "This is the guy, Captain," he said in almost a whisper, "the guy that won that giant lottery. It was – how many millions? – eighteen or something? Lotta good it does him now! You remember that don't you? He fired a shotgun at some reporters not long after to chase 'em away."

Frank remembered all right. Everyone did. Archie Deschamps-Lebeau had won the biggest lottery prize in history and had spent the time since trying to avoid the limelight that went with it.

"Yeah, I remember, Nick." Frank spoke softly, staring at the outline in the ice and snow where the body had lain face down. Two paramedics had carefully pried it up and rolled it over so that the lifeless eyes of Archie Deschamps-Lebeau were now staring at the gray afternoon sky.

"And I don't have to ask, do I, if you got all the pictures, since you decided to roll him over before I got here?" The annoyance in Frank's voice was clear. "And the measurements? What's the distance there between those indentations where his feet were in the ice? And what about that button over there? Is it his?"

"Hey, hey, Captain! Wait a minute!" Nick squatted down beside Frank, self-consciously waving his notebook. "We got everything. Anyway, we don't even know this is a homicide. There's no marks on the body. No signs of violence. Anybody else but this guy, we probably wouldn't even be here! The coroner's been and gone – by the way, she says there's no way she can do time of death for sure 'cause the old guy's been frozen." Nick lowered his voice. "And some of the guys here are freezing, Captain. Er ... you know what it's like. Some of them can't take the weather. They want to get going."

Frank looked up at the detective and grinned. "How come you never wear a hat, Nick? No! Don't answer that! I don't want to know!" He stood up and pulled down his own hat again. "Okay, let's get out of here. Incidentally," he nodded at the body, "who found him here?"

"His two daughters." Nick relaxed a bit and opened his notebook again as they walked toward their cars. "They dropped in on him every second day to see that he was okay. He had a bad heart. But that's as much company as he put up with. Apparently they came and made him lunch and then cooked things for him and put it in a freezer. Cleaned the place a bit. Stuff like that. They're the only ones he ever let into the house. The neighbors confirm that. The daughters were here last time and everything was all right. Today they show up and he's nowhere around. They go looking, figuring he's caught the big one. Sure enough, here he was out at the end of the backyard."

The two policemen had reached their cars as Nick finished talking. Frank got into his, started it, and turned the heater on full blast before getting out again. "Nick," he said, "these two daughters. They in pretty good shape?"

"What do you mean?" Nick wanted to know.

"Like, husky," Frank said, "strong. Do you think they could have carried the old guy out here by themselves and dumped him, say if he were dead, or maybe if he had a heart attack but wasn't quite dead and they wanted the weather to finish him off?"

Nick looked surprised. "Well, yeah, one of them in fact probably could do it all by herself. Why? You think they did it?"

Frank nodded. "Sure looks that way," he said.

What has led Captain Frank Ricketts to suspect the two daughters of Archie Deschamps-Lebeau of murder?

Solution on page 189

20

Spy Versus Spy

"In counterespionage, Hauptmann August, we are not interested in spies as much as we are in spy *networks*."

"I understand, Herr Oberst, but ..." Ernst August tried to break in, but it was Oberst Dietrich Staat's favorite lecture, and he was not about to have its delivery interrupted by an officer of inferior rank.

"So if we act upon your suggestion, Hauptmann," he continued, "we will succeed in doing what? We will arrest this ... this Kopenick of yours, and what will we have? Nothing but another foot soldier, another pair of eyes and ears that can be replaced just like that!" Oberst Staat snapped his fingers. It was a constant habit of his, one he indulged in almost as frequently as asking himself rhetorical questions.

Hauptmann Ernst August yielded to the defeat that crept from the back of his brain, ran over his skull, and fixed his face in an immobile, neutral expression. There was no other way but to endure it. He had been through this lecture before: the same words, the same intonations, the same gestures. The same stinking cloud of cigarette smoke. It made him wonder yet again what devious gremlin of fate had conspired to have him transferred from the Abwehr, the military intelligence service led by his hero, Admiral Canaris, to the Sicherheitdienst, the infamous SD. It was bad enough that he had to admit to his fellow career officers in the Wermacht that he was now working for that madman, Heydrich. Worse was that his superior officer was Dietrich Staat, the most short-sighted drone in the service.

Staat's lecture went on. "Stuttgart is full of little traitors like your Kopenick, full of closet communists. I understand your enthusiasm and I commend it. Your skill, too, in identifying Kopenick. But what does he mean to us?" The colonel paused to squash out his Gauloise and insert another into the end of his ivory cigarette holder. He did not offer one to August. "It may mean one less instrument in the network for a very short while. But before long, he will be replaced. No, in counterespionage we must ask ourselves ..."

Staat made an elaborate show of lighting the fresh cigarette with a table lighter on his desk. "You realize of course, Hauptmann, what would be of interest, what would be most useful ..." Staat had forgotten the question he was going to ask and inadvertently almost got right to the point, "... what would be most useful would be to find out who Kopenick's *cutout* is. Now. What would that do for us?"

Ernst August swallowed noisily. He was struggling to keep his mouth shut. The last time he'd endured this lecture, which was during the second time he had reported Kopenick's activities, Staat had laboriously explained "cutout" to him, as though both did not already know well that a cutout's role was to act as a protective connection between an agent and various subagents. The practice preserved security for the agent since, most of the time, a subagent never even learned the identity of his or her agent.

"If we knew who the cutout is, we could follow him. And then! And *then!*" Staat was reaching a plateau in his monologue. Ernst knew that either he would end it here, or God forbid, branch out in another direction. Before either could happen, Hauptmann Ernst August jumped in.

"Most astute as usual, Herr Oberst. You see, I know who the cutout is. Also, I know how they communicate. If you want to see them together and see how Kopenick passes the messages, we will have to go now while it is raining. If their pattern remains as consistent as it has been, they will rendezvous shortly near the Stiftskirche. At 1730 hours."

Luckily for Ernst August, his outburst coincided with one of Staat's elaborate inhalings. The officer core had been very much influenced in its smoking habits of late by French movies. But what Staat had just heard stopped all the mannerisms. And the lecture.

"You have his cutout?" The Oberst did not realize his mouth was agape.

"Yes, Oberst Staat. His name is Traugott Waechter. Swiss. At least he has a Swiss passport."

"Aha, a Swiss passport! Now what does that mean? It means ..."

"Yes, Herr Oberst. He travels back and forth once a week. Stuttgart to Bern. I suspect that it is because of this Waechter that you – that we have not been successful with the radio location equipment. I believe that in Stuttgart, at least, *Rote Kapelle* makes very little use of radios. With Waechter available as a courier, there is no need."

For the very first time, Oberst Dietrich Staat was silent. His mouth stayed open, but there were no words. His cigarette burned away unnoticed at the end of the holder. The mention of *Rote Kapelle* often had that effect on German intelligence.

To the SD and the Abwehr, and the Gestapo, too, the *Rote Kapelle* or "Red Orchestra" was a cause of profound embarrassment. It was a highly successful Soviet operation, a network that, especially in the first years of the war, sent amazingly accurate, thorough, and extensive reports to Moscow on German war production, military maneuvers, and even some of the long-range planning of the general staff. Many of the agents at the bottom of the chain – subagents – were ideological communists, a great number of them German, some Swiss, and some, like Kopenick, Czechs from the Sudetenland.

On two previous occasions, Ernst August's reports about Kopenick to Staat had stirred no response, a result he attributed to the continuing jealousy between the Abwehr and the SD. This time, what he offered Staat stimulated commitment to the common cause.

The commitment, or else the irresistible pleasure of wounding the Red network, boosted August over another hurdle with Staat, too. The two men were now sitting outside the Stiftskirche in August's somewhat battered, three-year-old Volkswagen. Staat had wanted to use his chauffeured Mercedes-Benz, but the captain had convinced him of the need for a small car, because to score their coup with Waechter and Kopenick they would likely have to maneuver through the medieval section of the city with its narrow streets and alleys.

They had arrived in the square in front of the Stiftskirche at 1728 hours and were lucky enough to be able to back into a parking space that concealed them from the street. Kopenick appeared at 1729 hours, making August look very good indeed. He stopped in front of the main entrance to the church for about thirty seconds, then drove off.

"Good! Where's the cutout? Why aren't we following?" Staat said through a thick cloud of cigarette smoke.

"He will be back." It occurred to Ernst for only the first time that Staat probably had no street experience at all. He was just an administrator. "They communicate with their cars," he added.

"Their cars?" Staat was asking questions to which he did not have a ready answer planned. Real questions. Ernst liked that.

"Do you see the little truck across the square? The plumber?" Ernst deliberately pressed on before Staat could answer. He knew the colonel had not noticed the truck. "That's Waechter. He uses different vehicles, but I've seen this one twice before. He also uses a ... ah, here's Kopenick again!"

Both men watched as the *Rote Kapelle* subagent drove into the square in his tiny, black Renault. This time he did not even stop but drove straight through.

"He's waiting for the traffic to pick up just a bit more," Ernst explained. "The more traffic, the more vehicles, the better for them. But they're running out of time, I think. Waechter can't sit there much longer without attracting attention."

Almost on top of his words, Kopenick reappeared. This time, Waechter pulled out into traffic ahead of him. August accelerated out of the parking space and over the next block slipped the Volkswagen in behind Waechter's truck. Within a few seconds, in what to anyone else would appear to have been natural traffic flow and interchange, the Renault was directly in front of Waechter. The three vehicles moved in single file that way for the next block.

"At the stop ahead," Ernst said. "That's where it'll start." Staat said nothing but smoked furiously as the line of cars slowed.

"Now! See!" Ernst August could not suppress his excitement. Or his righteousness. "See the message being sent? In Morse! Clumsy, but right in front of our noses! There!"

He translated excitedly.

"Bomb site – No! – *sight* ... man ... man ... must be manufacture – Yes! *manufacture* – moved to Ess ... Ess ... *Esslingen!* What did I tell you! 'Bombsight manufacture moved to Esslingen.' They get ..."

"Hauptmann! They're moving!"

In his excitement, Ernst had almost forgotten he was driving.

"Now wait till we stop again, Herr Oberst, and you'll see more! At this one, perhaps you will read the message for us. I can't stay right behind Waechter too long. He's a careful one!"

Dietrich Staat was exuding extreme discomfort and Hauptmann Ernst August basked in it. He knew the colonel had no idea what was going on.

"What's the matter, Oberst, is it the Morse?"

"Of course not!" the commanding officer snapped. "I know Morse! It's ... I don't ... I'm not ... *How do you know it's Morse?*"

The Abwehr captain rolled his window down slightly to let some of the smoke out, then took even more time in an elaborate assessment of whether the ensuing draft caused any discomfort for his superior. Only after he'd stretched the situation to the fringes of bad manners did he reply.

"Under the truck, Oberst Staat. Look under the truck."

? **What has Hauptmann Ernst August discovered? How are Kopenick and Traugott Waechter communicating in Morse code?**

Solution on page 190

21

The Search for Olie Jorgensson

The instant Detective-Sergeant Connie Mount signaled the little team behind her to halt and take a short break, they all turned to a patch of wild raspberries that grew in profusion at the edge of the trail and began to eat greedily. It was just one more thing that upset her about this search and rescue mission. The searchers were supposed to lie flat and relax totally to conserve their strength; there might be many miles to cover yet and there was plenty of daylight left.

Connie's uneasiness had been growing steadily from the very second this whole affair had started. That was at 7:03 a.m. this morning, when she walked into the Healey Lake detachment office where she was commanding officer. The night dispatcher, "Lefty" Shaw, still had a half hour left on his shift. He was standing at his desk with his finger on the PLAY button of the answering machine. Connie heard only the very last part of the tape, but she recognized the voice in spite of the panic in it.

"... don't know how long ago but he isn't anywhere on the campsite! We've looked everywhere! Won't you please hurry! He's so little!"

"That was Svena Jorgensson, wasn't it Norman?" Connie said.

She was the only one in the detachment – in the entire community – who didn't call him "Lefty"; she felt it kept him on his toes. Police work – his job – became secondary in Lefty's life whenever he was able to lay his hands on a new, or rather, a new *old* car. Lefty was a collector of classics and two days ago a 1912 Reo had made him completely forget why he was being paid a salary.

"Before you tell me all about it, *Norman,* why is her call on the answering machine instead of on your backup tape? This means you weren't at your desk, were you?"

Lefty's normally ruddy countenance glowed a notch brighter at Connie's challenge. "I had to go to the can!" he said indignantly. "It happens from time to time, you know!"

Connie nodded. "I suppose so. Nature, right?" She took a step forward and pressed REWIND on the answering machine. "You know, that reminds me. It's certainly time those washrooms were cleaned. Especially if we've got to get rid of that Number 90 gear grease you managed to get all over yourself when you were in there."

Lefty turned full red this time but Connie didn't notice. By now she'd punched PLAY and was listening to Svena Jorgensson tell the detachment that her little Olie was missing from their campsite at the lake. As far as she, Svena, knew, he'd gotten up while she was still asleep and wandered off and out into the bush. Olie was only four years old.

That had happened six hours ago, and although Connie had put together a full search and rescue response within forty-five minutes, she still felt that the whole thing might be just a wild goose chase; there were so many things that weren't right to begin with, and so many things that turned out wrong as they went along.

For one, the armed forces helicopter she'd called in to fly over the area with a heat sensor turned out to be a waste of time. There were simply too many wild animals in the area and their body heat made the sensor work like a popcorn machine. The system worked better as the helicopter flew some miles farther from the lake, but there was no point to that because it would have been impossible for a child Olie's age to get that far away in six hours.

The tracking dogs caused another problem. One was a Shepherd, the other a Blue Tick hound that Connie had worked with once before. Both dogs led their handlers directly to an abandoned railway line several hundred yards from the Jorgenssons' campsite. At that point, the animals disagreed. The Shepherd circled and circled and then simply sat down as if to say, "That's it. End of trail." The Blue Tick bounded down the former railway line in complete confidence, enthusiastically dragging the handler and the search team after him. But then he stopped, too, and like the Shepherd, circled a few times and sat down.

By this time, it was 11 a.m., and the August sun was heating up everyone's nerves, not least Connie's. It was at that point that, against her better judgement, certainly against her best instincts, she let Willy Stefan take over. Not that Willy was incompetent. On the contrary, he was regarded – and rightly so – as the best tracker the area had ever seen. Local wags loved to explain to tourists how Willy could track a mosquito through a swamp. But Willy was not exactly a neutral party in this case. He was Olie's uncle, Svena's brother-in-law, and in the Jorgensson family, that meant complications. Svena and her former husband were involved in a frightfully bitter and ongoing custody dispute over little Olie. That's why Connie had immediately recognized the voice on the answering machine. Olie's father regularly failed to bring him back after "visit" times. Once, the father, with the help of his sister and her husband, Willy, had snatched Olie out of the backyard of the Jorgensson home and had taken him away for two weeks.

These contradictions and complications had been rumbling away in the back of Connie's mind as the search team followed Willy Stefan at a respectable distance down the railway line. Now he stood, after she had called a halt, waiting for her to catch up.

Willy wiped the back of his neck with a peach-colored cloth that said Dunn & Dunn Service. "Slow going," he commented, giving expression to yet another burr that Connie was feeling. They had been moving at a snail's pace all along.

"Tourist season," Willy added as though that explained everything. He held the cloth at the corners and made it flap before wiping his face with it. "There's just so many people hiking along here this time of year," he said through the cloth. "Makes it so hard to read the signs. No wonder the dogs got mixed up."

Connie's reaction was instant. "That does it!"

She turned and yelled back to the others. "You people! I want you to go back a bit. Back up. Go around the curve and wait there till I call."

"Now, Willy," she lowered her voice. "You and I are going to talk. No. Strike that! *You* are going to talk. Talk a lot and talk fast! I want to know where that little boy is!"

Why does Connie Mount believe that Willy Stefan has something to tell her?

Solution on page 191

22

Murder at the David Winkler House

Chris Beadle paused in the narrow hallway and looked back at the doorway she'd just come through. Her height was average, yet she'd still had to duck.

"Atmosphere," she said out loud to no one in particular. "Anything for pioneer effect. But then ... why not?"

There was more pioneer effect right in front of her, for the door into the inn's only public washroom was just as small and would be sure to make a patron stoop. In fact, everything about the David Winkler House was small: the rooms, the halls, the doorways, the windows. But with clever restorations, the place seemed far more dainty than cramped. The David Winkler House had been built in the late eighteenth century by David Winkler – no surprise there – to accommodate his large family at a time when people were smaller than they are today. The present owners, the four innkeepers who had turned it into an extremely successful country dining room and inn, had been careful to preserve everything they could to make the place as authentic as possible.

From the moment Chris had left the graveled parking lot,

which was quite carefully and deliberately separated from the building by a row of lilac bushes and a profusion of hollyhocks in full bloom, she had felt herself slide backward in time. The owners had done such a good job. From the squeaky gate in the stockade fence to the milk paint on the shutters to the weathered cedar shingles on the roof, the David Winkler House spoke "authentic." And it spoke "charm."

They had succeeded inside, too. Only someone who looked carefully for them would ever find electrical outlets or switches or wires. There was no evidence of a telephone anywhere, not even where the hostess greeted the guests. Even the washroom, where Chris now stood, was hidden away from the dining area. It couldn't be found without asking. Not easily, anyway.

Chris ducked and stepped inside, remembering why she'd come back here in the first place. There wasn't much room. Not only was it a unisex facility, it barely accommodated one person at a time. She pushed the door open right to the wall. It just cleared a sink styled in antique porcelain that stood on a thin pedestal in the corner ahead of her and to the left. On the wall opposite the door hung a framed mirror, surrounded by dried roses, dried fern, and Queen Anne's lace. To her right, the unavoidable stark modernity of the toilet was softened by an identical mirror on the wall above it, this one holding up a tangle of green foxtail. In a deliberate sequence, Chris flushed the toilet, turned each tap on, then off, and gently pushed the door closed.

"Not bad," she said, again out loud but to no one in particular. It was impossible to make a washroom look eighteenth century, certainly in what had been a pioneer home. But everything was designed for silence. The door did not squeak, and the plumbing was absolutely hushed. No modern noises to intrude on the atmosphere.

On the remaining wall hung the sampler that Kate Mistoe said she was nailing up when Menelaus Atko was shot. It was a delicately embroidered piece of work, set in a frame similar to that used for the mirrors. It didn't have the familiar proverb or Biblical quotation, however. This sampler held another oblique intrusion from the twentieth century. What it said, in very fine needlework, was:

O, Winkler patrons, please take heed
These things our septic does not need.

A most unpoetic list of the jetsam of modern living followed: matches, cigarette butts, napkins, hairpins, aluminum foil. Chris counted nineteen items that Winkler patrons were not to throw into the toilet!

Kate Mistoe had been here in the washroom when Menelaus Atko was shot in the dining room earlier this morning. Or so she said. Her story was supported, though, by Sandy Sanchez. Sandy's account was that he was going past the washroom on his way to the propane tanks out back at the time the shots were fired. He and Kate had stared at each other for what seemed like forever, frozen in shock and fear. Then they wasted more precious time colliding with each other in the narrow hallway in their effort to get to the dining room where they found the body of Menelaus, bleeding but not breathing. Through the window, both swore they'd seen a blue car roar onto the road from the parking lot in a plume of gravel and exhaust.

That part of the story was verified in turn by Karl Schloss who had been driving up the road to the David Winkler House from the opposite direction. He'd seen the blue car turn to the right in a skid at the intersection a short distance away, and then disappear. The dust from the gravel, according to Schloss, along with the exhaust, hung like a trail over the parking lot and down the road. Schloss had run into the dining room to find Sanchez and Mistoe clinging to each other, as far from the late Menelaus Atko as they could get.

All three, Mistoe, Sanchez and Schloss, were now sitting in the kitchen waiting for Chris to finish her walkabout. To her, they were still prime suspects, in spite of the story of the blue car and the fact that their alibis all dovetailed so neatly.

Chris had questioned them separately an hour before. Schloss's story would be the easiest to check. He said he'd been in town at a service station getting the oil changed in his car. Normally that would make his alibi entirely solid, but there was a hitch. He had not come directly back to the Winkler House but had detoured via one of the farms where the inn bought fresh produce each day. When he saw that there was no one home there, he'd left and arrived back at the David Winkler House just in time to see the blue car speed away.

Sandy Sanchez, during his interview, had been exceptionally animated. As he spoke, his hands were constantly on the move in sweeping, dramatic gestures. The fittings on the propane tanks needed tightening, he'd said, making big round clockwise circles at Chris with his fist, as though he were holding a wrench. It was while he was on his way to do that when he and Kate heard the shots.

Chris felt the man's animated style was natural; he probably talked that way all the time. In any case it would be easy enough to verify. So would his knowledge of propane systems. What bothered her most was that his story supported Kate Mistoe's, and it meant then that both were lying. So then what about Schloss? Was there a three-way conspiracy here at Winkler House?

One thing she had to do right away was talk to Atko's lawyer. The three prime suspects each owned ten percent of the inn. Atko held the rest. What she wanted to know was what kind of in-the-event-of-death clause there was in their partnership agreement. If Mistoe, Schloss and Sanchez stood to gain substantially from their late partner's death, then ...

?

Why does Chris Beadle believe that Kate Mistoe and Sandy Sanchez are lying? Why does she want to find out what Sandy Sanchez knows about propane systems? And how can she check out Karl Schloss's story?

Solution on page 192

23

Incident on the Picket Line

12 October

Memorandum

To: Yvonne Hawkins, Manager of Claims,
        Belwood Insurance Company

From: Eileen Cook, Claims Investigator

This is my preliminary report on the claim by Mr. Roger Monk of Roger Monk Transport Limited, for damage to his tractor-trailer.*

Mr. Monk is the owner-driver of the following vehicle: a diesel-powered, cab-over-engine style Freightliner tractor with a rear tandem axle. The cab has a sleeper compartment attached. The trailer is a flatbed type, with a single rear axle. Complete specifications for the vehicle will be in the appendix to my final report.

The police report states that ten days ago, on October 2, Mr. Monk

---

* Please note that Mr. Monk is British, and describes the vehicle in his own claim as an "articulated lorry." The police refer to it as a semi.

drove his tractor-trailer to the entrance gate of the Agromax Farm Machinery Company. He acknowledges that he was aware of a strike at Agromax, and that there had been several incidents of violence on the picket line. However, he contends that because his trailer was empty, he felt that the picketers would let him through unchallenged.

As Mr. Monk drove to the gate, members of the picket line set upon his equipment, presumably causing the damage listed in his claim. The police report confirms that during the incident both exhaust stacks were damaged beyond repair, along with the windshield and both headlamps. It also confirms that every single tire was slashed, so that both tractor and trailer had to be towed away after order was restored. Also, a striker entered the sleeper compartment and had to be forcibly removed. A complete copy of the police report is being sent to your attention.

Roger Monk has listed the following in his claim:
- towing charges
- complete repainting of the tractor
- replacement of the windshield and two headlamps
- replacement of two exhaust stacks
- replacement of sixteen tires
- replacement of one set of bagpipes.

My recommendations are as follows:

One: that the towing charges be paid immediately.

Two: that the repainting of the tractor be negotiated. This tractor is four years old, and the need for painting is at least partly the result of normal wear and tear.

Three: that damaged parts be replaced only if confirmed in the police report.

Four: The bagpipes are a special problem. According to police, a striker did indeed enter the sleeping compartment during the incident, but there is no independent confirmation that it was the striker who damaged the bagpipes, or that the bagpipes were even in the sleeper.

My recommendation is that the company decline to pay for them in view of the fact that there is already an attempt at fraud in this claim.

My full report will follow in two days.

Respectfully,
Eileen Cook

?   **What is the attempt at fraud that Eileen Cook refers to?**

Solution on page 193

Footprints on the Trail

Torrey Mazer had made it to the top of the Criminal Investigation Branch for one very simple reason. She was a darn good cop. She knew it, too, as did the people in her department, which explained why there was never a hint of resentment from inside the force. Even when she encountered the inevitable smart remarks from people on the outside, her self-confidence always helped her to ignore it. However, what Torrey did not deal with very well was the fact that she was short. So short that her personnel file carried the minutes of an appeal meeting on the matter of her height held when she was a cadet-in-training fifteen years before. A physical education instructor had made the mistake of refusing to graduate her from his course, claiming she was too tiny to meet his standards.

In fact, Torrey topped the height requirements with even a bit to spare. But her legs were abnormally short and made her appear small. This was one point on which the male officers in her department showed no mercy. Though she could never prove it, Torrey knew that none of them ever *walked* with her. They took strides. Big ones, stretched to the limit so that she had to almost canter to keep up. Yet she could never bring herself to say anything, so that "almost cantering" became her on-duty style.

At the moment, just behind and to the right of Constable Wally Harris, Torrey Mazer was cantering as usual – and she was more than a little embarrassed about it, too. She wasn't helped at all by the terrain. The rough, frozen field they were crossing was covered with flattened weeds and scrub brush that snagged at her feet and at the edges of her bulky overcoat. It had been a cold but snowless winter, bleak and ugly. Everything in the field was gray and dirty brown.

"We're coming right up to it now, Inspector," Wally Harris said over his right shoulder. "You can see there's some smoke still rising on the other side of the hill just ahead. If the wind was in our faces, the smell would gag you. We're lucky today."

The smell Wally referred to came from the charred bodies of thousands of turkeys that had died in a barn fire two days before. The Criminal Investigation Branch was involved because it had been a clear case of arson. Clumsy arson, too, but successful because of a terrible coincidence. Just before the fire, in a first promise of spring, a day and night of mild thaw had prompted the turkey-farm owners to move extra stock into the barn from other buildings. Thus the number of turkeys burned was much larger than it might have been. By the time the alarm was called in just before dawn, Mother Nature had suddenly reversed herself. The temperature plunged so fast that when the fire trucks arrived, the hose connections at the farm had to be loosened with torches. The delay had been costly.

Torrey doubled her cantering speed and caught up to Wally Harris just as they crested the hill. Then both of them stopped abruptly. It wasn't so much the sight of the smoldering ruin below them as it was the odor. Vile, pungent and penetrating. Neither officer made any pretense about covering their faces.

"Normally we could go down right here, Inspector," Wally said.

"But the footprints we came to see are over there." He pointed to a very steep hill on their left that ran straight down to the edge of what had been the barn. "The path is on that hill," Wally continued. "It goes from the barn up over the hill to an equipment shed. The path is so steep, they only use it in summer. It's a shortcut. Anyway, the footprints are there. It's pretty obvious that whoever torched the barn came down that path and set up with a slow-burning fuse, but, uh, Inspector, I think you're gonna see it can't really be Tibor Nish who made those footprints."

Torrey had come to the site to see for herself a set of footprints that may or may not belong to Tibor Nish who, for the present, was the only suspect. On the path down the hill, investigators had found a set of footprints made by a pair of size twelve Kodiak work boots. Tibor Nish not only wore size twelve Kodiaks, he had been dismissed by the turkey farm for drunkenness only a week before the fire. Nor did Nish deny that his footprints might be on the trail. He said he had returned to pick up a pair of coveralls four days ago. When he couldn't find them in the equipment shed, he went to look in the barn. He had used the path down to the barn because he was in a hurry, knowing he was not welcome on the farm. He'd found the coveralls, then hurried out the front gate. Another farm worker had seen Tibor Nish at the barn. She did not think it was four days ago, but rather, on the day *before* the fire, in the late afternoon. When pressed, however, she admitted she couldn't be absolutely sure.

Torrey could see the footprints in question easily, even before she and Wally came up the path. A single set of tracks leading down the hill. They were from big shoes all right, stamped into the middle of the path. The indentations were clear, especially deep at the heel. Kodiaks without question.

"Well," Torrey began, straightening up after a close look at the prints, "it's going to be pretty hard for Tibor Nish to explain these.

My guess is if we lean on him a little he'll admit his guilt. Lucky for him nobody died in that fire."

Wally's face reddened. His lips shaped a number of words before he finally spoke. "But inspector." He put his own feet beside the footprints and took a step down the hill. "Nish has got ... Nish has got...." Wally found this hard to say. "Nish has got long legs," he finally blurted. "Longer than me even. He's taller than me. These footprints. They're so close together. Watch." He took a step that easily covered two of the paces showing in the frozen ground. "Whoever made these prints must have, well, *really short legs!*"

By now, Wally's face was far redder than a cold winter's day could make it.

"Wally," Torrey was being very patient. "Trust me. I'll give you any odds you want, that it was Nish. Let's walk down to the barn, slowly and I'll explain."

? **Why is Inspector Torrey Mazer so certain that the footprints have been made by the suspect, Tibor Nish?**

Solution on page 193

25

A Very Brief Non-Interview

The office was ultra modern, a place of hums. A hum came through the air-conditioning grate above the door. A double bank of fluorescent lighting hummed in the ceiling. Over in one corner, a computer hummed in droning, flat counterpoint to the spectacular, silent flowerbursts that looped in random delight on the screen.

Sheila Lacroix stood quietly in the midst of the hums. She could hear them, but paid no attention. There were too many other things to take in. The desk, just a few steps in front of her, was bulky silent, imposing, and impeccably neat. Bookshelves on the wall to her left were filled with leatherbound volumes standing in silent, parade-ground readiness against the time when a user might have need of them. Below the shelves, a selection of newspapers was arranged carefully across a table. Sheila made a quick estimate; there were twenty different issues at least.

Across from her, and beyond the desk, the wall was glass from floor to ceiling, the panes set in almost invisibly narrow frames. She might have been on the 22nd floor of any office building in New York, London, Geneva, or Toronto.... Except for the newspapers. The

New York and London *Times* were in the lineup all right, and out of the corner of her eye Sheila could see *Zeitung* on one of the mastheads. But the majority of the headlines were in Arabic. The view through the window told her where she was, too. Without moving her head, Sheila could count five of the mosques in central Amman.

But most especially, what told her – what would tell anyone – she was not in a western country was the very tall man bending over a tiny table near the remaining wall. He was turned away from Sheila, and except for the hand resting on the back of his hip, an incredibly long index finger pointing at the windows, she could not see any part of him as he was entirely covered by his pristine white, flowing *thobe*, and over that a shorter *aba* in desert brown. The tall man, whose other hand was furiously signing documents, was Ibrahim Jamaa, leader of the Brotherhood of the Eternal Light of Allah. It was he whom Sheila Lacroix had come to see.

"Now don't stare at him, whatever you do!" Sheila could remember every one of the attaché's instructions clearly. "As a matter of fact, don't make eye contact at all, or for more than a second or two. He knows you're western so he'll forgive you a glance, but ...," he shrugged, "you're a woman. Hey, I don't make the rules! This is Jordan, not Saskatchewan."

It had struck Sheila at the time that the attaché was exceptionally world-weary for one so young. "I have no idea how you did this," the young man had said, shaking his head. "No one – like, literally *nobody* – from any of the embassies has ever seen this guy close up; his organization is fanatical about secrecy – probably about a few other things, too! We've tried to get in here for months with no success, and here he gives you an appointment just like that!" He lifted his hand to snap his fingers for emphasis but then decided such behavior would be undiplomatic.

Sheila wanted to point out quite firmly that a year of traveling and beating on doors and shouting and bribing and threatening was hardly "just like that." Fourteen months ago, her husband had been kidnapped, presumably for political reasons, somewhere in Haseke province in Syria, where the border meets Iraq and Turkey. Bill Lacroix was a doctor working there with Kurdish refugees. From the time of his disappearance until now, not a single one of the Middle Eastern groups known to use kidnapping for political purposes would acknowledge they held him.

Sheila had let the Canadian Department of External Affairs prove itself useless before striking out on her own. Since then, although she was only vaguely aware of it, she was probably the only western non-diplomat and non-journalist to speak personally to the leadership of Black September, Hamas, the PLO, even the PPK. All of them had denied any knowledge of Bill Lacroix. Now Sheila was about to score the most significant coup of all, in the eyes of the diplomats anyway; she was about to speak directly to Ibrahim Jamaa of the Eternal Light of Allah.

"Don't speak first under any circumstances." The attaché had been full of advice. "You let him initiate the conversation. Somehow you've got to make it seem like you're answering *his* questions rather than the other way around."

"And ... and ..." The flow stopped suddenly. "... Uh ... there's one more thing, Mrs. Lacroix, if you would?" For a few seconds, the attaché's diplomatic mask came off. "We ... we know nothing about this Ibrahim Jamaa. We're not even absolutely sure what he looks like. One thing we know is that he's very tall. Unusually so, like, really basketball-tall! He wears a patch over his right eye; we know that. Speaks perfect English. Italian and German, too."

"So I'm supposed to bring you his birth certificate and his wedding album?" Sheila had long ago lost patience with External Affairs.

"No, no, no!!" The attaché reddened. "You see – and I'm being very frank with you here – what we have about him comes from the CIA and Mossad." He looked over Sheila's shoulder. "We really don't have a lot of faith in them anymore. So if there's anything that you see that is, well, *interesting*, we would like to know. Please?"

Sheila had taken one step into the elevator when he rushed to her and pulled her back gently. "One more thing we know. I don't really believe it would have anything to do with the whereabouts of Dr. Lacroix, but ... Jamaa professes to be *mujtahid*. Means he's sort of a freethinker, especially about religion. Now the Shiites generally go along with that, but the Sunnis don't, and since Jordan is about eighty percent Sunni, that could make him a bit unwelcome here."

Standing in the office only a few minutes later, while Ibrahim Jamaa continued to write, helped Sheila understand all too well what it felt like to be unwelcome. However, when the man finally turned to face her, she forgot the feeling altogether. It was replaced by a sense of overwhelming menace that she knew would stay with her for a long time.

He was tall, all right, possibly seven feet, but that could be, Sheila later reflected, because of his power, his presence. Ibrahim Jamaa would have been a tower of malevolence at only six feet. He turned to her in what seemed like slow motion. First the patch appeared. Black, set in deep creases on the cheekbone. It was so striking that the rest of his face, Sheila was convinced, followed with abnormal slowness.

Despite herself, she stared. First at the patch, then at the single dark eye that appraised her without a flicker of response. Only when he brought his fingertips together in front of his chest – the incredibly long index finger had a matching partner – in what was just barely a gesture of greeting, did Sheila take her eyes away.

Jamaa took a step, then another. It brought him to the edge of the desk.

"Mrs. Lacroix," he said. Then there was silence. Sheila was suddenly aware of the hums again. She dared to glance up at the face and then looked down. The single eye still revealed nothing.

"Mrs. Lacroix," he said again. The attaché was correct about the English. Not a trace of an accent.

Sheila watched a long index finger as it tapped, first the edge of the desk, then the shoulder cradle attached to the telephone. He appeared to be searching for the right words. The finger traced the slim, arching neck of a desk lamp. The man was clearly used to commanding long silences while others waited for him to speak.

"Your husband ..."

Finally! The reason she was there! She was surprised the subject was broached so quickly.

"... Your husband," he repeated. "The doctor. We have no interest in him. Our organization does not interfere with the work of medical relief. We seek only justice for true believers, the people who are thwarted in their search by the Zionist aggressors. I do not know where your husband is. The Brotherhood does not know where your husband is." Jamaa brought his fingertips together again in front of his chest and inclined his head ever so slightly. The interview – the *non*-interview – was over. He turned, slowly, and went back to the table where he had stood before.

Sheila had to pull her feet off the floor in order to turn and go out the door and across the hall to the elevators. She wasn't in the least surprised that the attaché got to his feet far more eagerly when the elevator doors opened than he had when they first met.

"What did you find out? What's he like?" He pressed in most undiplomatic style.

Sheila shook her head. "Nothing you'd be interested in. But it's a step ahead for me. The Brotherhood of the Eternal Light of Allah knows about my husband. They must."

"What makes you say that?" The young attaché was subdued, but curious.

"Because that was not Ibrahim Jamaa. Or if it was – which I doubt – that was not his office."

What has led Sheila Lacroix to this conclusion?

Solution on page 194

26

Murder at 12 Carnavon

Honey Spehr was upset. And whenever she became upset, the color would rise in her face. It would start beneath the formal collars she always wore in court, and then flush up her neck until her cheeks fairly beamed with a crimson hue. Right now she could feel them burning.

"Mrs. Spehr?" Judge Ellesmere was speaking to her. "Mrs. Spehr? Do you wish to cross-examine?"

"Your Honor." Honey cleared her throat and willed her cheeks to dim.

The judge spoke again, "Would you like a few minutes first, Mrs. Spehr?"

"Thank you, your Honor." Honey was relieved. Now at least she didn't have to *ask* for a recess. "That would be helpful. Unless my friend here objects."

She forced herself to look at Gilbey Barnett's attorney, for she knew that Todd Roland could see her cheeks, too.

Gary Ellesmere peered over his half-glasses. "Mr. Roland has no objection, I'm sure. Do you, counselor?"

It wasn't a question. His Honor was rather unsubtly re-clarifying the pecking order. Todd Roland had been occupying center stage very successfully all day, and Ellesmere didn't care for the perform-ance. Still, because Roland knew he was winning, the judge's arbi-trariness didn't bother him in the least. Why would it? The jury had been nodding in unison with him all morning.

"Of course not, Your Honor. I'd be happy to let Mrs. Spehr have as much time as she needs to ... ah ... as she needs."

"Very well." The judge jumped to his feet, causing all the court officers to scramble to theirs. "Fifteen minutes," he pronounced over his shoulder as he headed for his chambers.

From where she sat at the prosecuting attorney's table, Honey's law clerk, Marion Kent, wondered whether the real reason for the judge's unaccustomed sensitivity was that he had to go to the bath-room. She didn't have a chance to comment, however, for no sooner did she and Honey get to their own ready room when Honey let go.

"He's lying, that slime, and he's getting away with it! He killed that woman! I know it. You know it. Anybody who bothers to think knows it. But he and Roland have got that jury thinking he's Francis of Assisi!"

She began to pace, tapping the index and third fingers of one hand into the palm of the other with each step. The effect was calming.

"Somehow I've got to make that jury realize that Gilbey Barnett may be smooth all right, but underneath the enamel is a liar! The thing is ..." Honey's voice grew quieter, more deliberate. The rosy color was gone altogether now. "... The thing is ... *how?* We'll never swing that jury back to rational thinking now. Not with what we've got to offer!"

Marion wished Honey wouldn't use the first person plural. Like the jury, she had been quite impressed with Barnett's defense; she wasn't at all as convinced as Honey of the man's guilt. But then – she had often admitted this to herself – no one had Honey's "nose for phonies." Was Gilbey Barnett a phoney? Was he lying? Did he kill his wife? If anybody was ever going to find out, it would be Honey Spehr.

Her case had begun with a building superintendent whose testimony showed that Barnett kept a mistress. Then there was the late Mrs. Barnett's sister, who described the fighting between her brother-in-law and his wife. This was reluctantly corroborated by a member of the Barnetts' cleaning service.

Mrs. Barnett had been shot in the back of the head at close range with a .22 caliber pistol. No weapon had ever been found, but a smug little clerk from Records and Registrations had stood in the box long enough to hold up a registration card for a Smith and Wesson of that caliber. The name on the card was W. Gilbey Barnett.

A combination of testimonies from a forensic pathologist and a neighbor, who had seen Mrs. Barnett pick up the morning paper on the porch, established the time of death at between 10:20 a.m. and 11:40 a.m.

Honey's ace was Constable First Class Jeff Baldwin. She had called him last. ("Responded to a dispatch at 11:44 a.m.; a shooting at the rear of 12 Carnavon Boulevard.") Baldwin's notes were always impeccably precise. He had entered the sunporch at 12 Carnavon to find "the defendant standing over the deceased."

Despite the fact that no weapon was found, the smoking-gun impression that Baldwin left with the jury was very powerful. It was Honey's intent to show in final summation that the time frames, no matter what Barnett's alibis, were such that given all the other evidence, Gilbey Barnett was a guilty man.

Todd Roland, however, had a few surprises and they were very effective. To begin with he didn't cross-examine a single prosecution witness. A very chancy strategy, but if it works, one that creates the impression that these witnesses and their testimony are not really very important. It can also make the prosecution case seem short. Roland's second surprise was to call Barnett first, not last, as everyone expected, and his third was to ask Judge Ellesmere to clear the courtroom of all the subsequent witnesses. By then Honey knew what he was going to do but was powerless to stop it. Any objection would have strengthened his ploy.

Roland's strategy was to draw out Gilbey Barnett's own account first, replete with detail upon detail, then corroborate it piece by piece, bit by bit, inexorably, with a parade of witnesses, until it became concrete in the collective psyche of the jurors that the defendant simply had to be telling the truth.

Barnett acknowledged that, yes, he had a mistress and that, yes, his marriage had been in difficulty ("You see, I suspected my late wife of being a drug user and we argued a lot about that.")

Honey had leaped in with an objection because there was absolutely no proof of that, and Ellesmere sustained but it was too late. The idea was already planted in the jury. Roland managed to slip it in again as a reason for having a license for a gun ("I was sure she'd been consorting with some very shady people: drug people and that like.")

On the day of the murder, Barnett testified, he left for his office at 7:40 a.m. and left there in turn at 9:20 a.m. to have some breakfast at First Came the Egg ("You understand, she just wouldn't make breakfast anymore, so to avoid conflict I simply ate out.") He left the restaurant at precisely 10:30 a.m. ("How do I know that, Mr. Roland? Well, the waitress – poor thing, I felt so sorry for her – she was so busy that she tripped right by my table and spilled ketchup on me!") As he said that he turned and held his left leg out of the witness box as though to show the jury the stain was still there. That was when Honey's color began to rise fast for the jurors turned as one to look at the pant leg. *And they were nodding!*

Barnett finally got around to explaining his precise 10:30 departure by saying that this particular waitress had left the restaurant at the same time he did, and she had told him she only worked the early morning shift and was now going home to change clothes for her other job.

Then he went to Harry's Men's Shop for a final fitting on a suit. And that call was memorable because the tailor, who was normally so adept, stuck him with a pin ("right in the ketchup on my sock!").

After the fitting he left. ("I left at 11:10 a.m. How do I know? Oh, because I was late now. I wanted to go home to change clothes before my luncheon meeting and I looked at my watch. I had to get from Harry's to home and then to Le Coq d'Or by noon. It was going to be very tight.")

Barnett went on to testify he'd arrived at 12 Carnavon at about 11:40 ("I looked at my watch again at the top of the street") and that while going up the walk, he heard a shot at the back of the house. By the time he ran through the house, whoever had fired it was gone ("and I was just frozen there until Constable Baldwin found me just like he described").

The rest of Barnett's testimony went just like that: precise, unhesitating, completely forthcoming. Every time Roland backed him up to fill in a blank, the response came through as though it was scripted. Which in Honey's opinion, it was. She knew that by this time there was not a single juror who wasn't thinking dismissal. All they needed was some reinforcement to tip them into absolute certainty. And with the next witnesses, Roland gave them that in a flood of verifying details. That the main point was left essentially untreated – namely, that Roland had not shown at all that Barnett was elsewhere when the shot was fired – didn't matter. All the jury heard was how exact Barnett's testimony had been.

It began with the security guard at his office. ("Certainly I know

Mr. Barnett. Everyone does. He's so generous to all of us especially at Christmas. He ...")

"*Objection!*" Honey's objection had been so vigorous that it didn't even seem necessary for Ellesmere to sustain.

The guard went on to say that he signed Barnett in at 8:16 a.m. The secretary, who was up next, verified that he left at 9:20. ("No. Mr. Barnett didn't use to go out for breakfast, but for the past year he did all the time.") The waitress followed the secretary then, with testimony that Honey knew she'd never poke through. ("Oh, it was so embarrassing when I fell, but he's such a nice man ...")

Ellesmere looked at Honey. His face said: "Go ahead. Object. I'm getting sick of this, too!" But Honey knew it would turn the jury away from her even further.

The waitress went on to say that Barnett left with her at 10:30 ("I always leave at 10:30. I have another job at Ruskin's department store. It's hard when you're raising two kids all on your own with no help. Anyway he ...").

Roland shut her down quickly then and called the tailor. That's when Honey's hope sank altogether. The little tailor was right out of Central Casting! Short, bald, pudgy, the most benign face she had ever seen. The guy was a fairy godfather!

And he had an accent. No, not just an accent. A *cute* accent! ("I haf been thoaty yeeahs tailor. Harry's-a ma brother.) By now, Honey knew the jury was watching a movie. This was entertainment! That was when the color started to creep up her neck. The tailor pointed at Barnett. ("Yes. He's-a come ... oh ... ten-toaty, maybe ten-foaty.") Then he smiled. ("That's-a ma suit! Foaty-two tall. You like ... eh, Mistah Bahnett?") *Now the jury was laughing!* ("Dat morning. I'm-a rememba de ketchup. On da floor I kneel. Mesha da cuff, and-a there's-a ketchup on da sock.")

Wisely, Roland stopped him there. Although the jury was enjoying every minute, he could see that Judge Ellesmere's sense of humor had reached its limit. It wouldn't do to have the jury's mood blown away by a tirade.

Honey, on the other hand, was nearly apoplectic. That's when Ellesmere, instead of getting angry as well, called the recess. Now, in the ready room, Honey was trying to prepare herself to go back out. But to what? She knew that the jury was entirely in Barnett's camp. She knew that without doubt, in their room right now, they were regaling themselves trying to imitate the little tailor or clucking in sympathy with the waitress.

She knew that logic would not win them back. No matter how relentlessly she focused on the time frame and showed that Barnett *could* have made it from Harry's Men's Shop to his home in time to shoot his wife, nothing was going to penetrate the web of certainty that Roland had woven.

"The only way," she said to Marion, "the only possible way to make them listen to me is to break up that perfect story. I've got to show them they're being misled. The story's a layer cake; it's *manufactured*. If I can only show them one single contradiction then they'll listen, and we can go to work on the *real* evidence. Now we ... Oh! Marion! I almost missed it!"

The color began to rise again in Honey Spehr's cheeks, but this time there was a glint in her eye.

? **Honey has found the contradiction, she thinks, the crack in the carefully crafted defense that she needs to return the jury to rationality. What is it?**

Solution on page 195

27

The Case of Queen Isabella's Gift

Two monologues were fighting for attention in Geoff Dilley's brain. One was by Vicar Titteridge. He was talking about keys.

"Tourists would be entirely disappointed in these," he was saying as he took a pair of shiny brass keys from his pants pocket and inserted one into the padlock hanging from a hasp on the old church door.

"They much prefer this kind of thing, of course." He held up a worn leather thong in front of Geoff's face, dangling a huge, black iron key larger than his hand. "Interesting, what? Can't blame them, really, the tourists. A blacksmith made this quite some time before locksmiths and that sort of profession were ever heard of, you see."

Geoff wanted to point out that the Romans had padlocks, that the Chinese had used combination locks for centuries, and that in the Middle Ages locks were made that could count the number of times a key was inserted. But the vicar struck him as the type that was unaccustomed to contradiction.

"The key is almost two hundred years old, we think. Can't be proven, of course, but church records indicate the door here was replaced in the same year George IV became Prince Regent. You know, when his poor father went bonkers once and for all. At any rate, it's only logical to assume the key was made at the same time."

He rapped on the door firmly. "Solid oak this. From the New Forest. Very unusual that. Needed royal permission to cut the tree. Still, the door's a relative junior compared to the church itself: 1320 it was dedicated. Legend has it Edward II himself was here for the ceremony. Doesn't seem likely though, for it's sure that Queen Isabella was here. And you know about those two."

Geoff wanted to say that yes, he did know all about those two, but he didn't for the vicar had finally inserted the big key and turned it. The door opened easily and noiselessly, exposing the cool darkness inside. It occurred to Geoff that tourists would prefer some nice, authentic creaking, but he said nothing and waited in the doorway while the vicar stepped inside and turned on the lights.

"You'll have to come up to the altar," the vicar said. "The candelabra were up there."

"Candelabra" triggered the other monologue, the one Geoff Dilley had been trying to suppress. It came back again, though. Verbatim.

"*Candelabra!*" It was Chief Inspector Peddelley-Spens and he was shouting. "Bleedin' *candelabra?* We've got seven – count 'em, seven – homicide investigations going on at this precise moment. There's mad Irishman bombin' the country to bleedin' bits. I've got a bunch o' bleedin fox-kissers chained t' the fence at Marlborough Hunt. The bleedin' prime minister o' bleedin Portugal is comin' this afternoon. And *you!* You want to investigate the theft of a bleedin' pair o' candelabra?" Peddelley-Spens stopped to take in a huge breath. "I suppose that next you'll want the weekend off, too, so you can join hands with those frog-kissers that want a bleedin' tunnel under the bleedin' M5?"

Suddenly, the Chief Inspector had softened to half volume.

"One!" he said. "You can make one call!" And then to normal volume altogether. "Look, Geoff. I know how much you like bleedin' old things. But you're a good investigator. I need you here! Now you can trot off to – where is it? – St. Dunstan's-by-the-Water? But I want you back today before tea. Somebody's got to mind the crime rate while the rest of us are guardin' his Portuguese worship!"

Geoff's love of "bleedin' old things" – he had long ago despaired of instructing Peddelley-Spens in the use of "antiquarian" – made him more than anxious to visit St. Dunstan's-by-the-Water. He knew the ancient church but had never been in it. St. Dunstan's was a tiny but most unusual structure. A chapel really, rather than a church, but it was Norman and that made it special. Since it was built in the early fourteenth century, when Gothic architecture had wholly supplanted all other forms, St. Dunstan's lay claim to being the last piece of Norman architecture built in England.

In the hour it had taken him to drive there, Geoff came to realize he would never be able to make Peddelley-Spens appreciate just how valuable, how utterly priceless and irreplaceable the stolen candelabra really were.

"A gift of Queen Isabella," the vicar had said on the telephone. "You can still see her seal. Gold, of course. Each piece has some quite lovely stones, too."

Geoff knew that if the candelabra were not found right away, their fate would go one of two ways: they would either be fenced to a collector or, more likely, the stones would be pried out and the gold melted down. Either way, no one would ever see the ancient pieces again.

"Watch your step." The vicar's monologue returned just a shade too late to save Geoff from stumbling as they walked up the short aisle. "Original floors, you know. Even stone wears after six-and-a-half centuries."

Geoff had been following the vicar as slowly as possible so he could look around. He wanted to spend time in this church. It was Norman, all right. Thick walls, round arches, windows that looked more like arrow slits.

"Right there. Above the altar. They stood on those two pedestals."

Geoff stared at the altar.

"No, no. Higher. Up there." The vicar directed Geoff's gaze to a point well above the altar where two small stone platforms jutted out from the columns leading from the ends of the altar to the roof.

"I assume ..." the vicar was still talking. Other than introducing himself, Geoff had yet to say a word. "I assume he, or she – maybe even *they*. There were several dozen strangers here last night. Isn't it curious how we automatically believe it is males who commit crime? I assume the perpetrator, or perpetrators, attended Evensong last night and then hid in the church until it was empty. The candelabra were definitely here, for they were lit. Everyone saw them. They're only lit for Evensong. Too much of a bother, even with a step stool and extended candlelighters. And I assume that since we lock the main door on the outside as you saw, that he or she or they went out here."

The vicar led Geoff to a door behind the altar. "It's the only other way in or out," he said. "A concession to the twentieth century. Fire regulations and all that, you see."

He leaned against the crash bar, covering the little, red and silver sign that said "Emergency Exit Only" with his bottom, and opened the door. Geoff followed him outside and turned to watch the door close and lock automatically.

"When I'm alone, I normally enter this way." The vicar produced the pair of brass keys again and opened the door. "Less fuss. Did so this morning."

Geoff followed the vicar back inside.

"Really don't know what made me look up. At any rate they were gone, and straight away I rushed back out and telephoned you."

For the first time, Geoff opened his mouth and was actually going to speak, but the vicar anticipated his question and beat him to it. "You're going to ask me about the verger, aren't you? Well, we don't have one at St. Dunstan's. Poor old Albert died over a year ago, and we never arranged for a replacement. This is only a chapel, really. A Sunday morning service and then Evensong, so there's no need. One of the parishioners comes every second Tuesday. I let her in and we clean together."

Geoff took a breath and got out "How ..." before the vicar said, "There were between forty and fifty last night. About fifteen regulars. No, no. This way."

Geoff had turned to go out behind the altar.

"So we can turn the lights out and double lock the main door again. Pity we have to do that. House of God and all that, but then I certainly don't have to tell you about it. The crime rate, I mean."

The vicar paused to straighten a hymn book, and Geoff blurted, "No, Vicar. I know all about it." The voice of Peddelley-Spens rumbled like distant thunder in the back of his mind. "But it's even worse when a man of the cloth adds to it. The crime rate, I mean."

Why has Geoff Dilley concluded that Vicar Titteridge has stolen the pair of candelabra?

Solution on page 196

28

Quite Possibly, the Annual Meeting of the Ambiguity Society

Normally, being assigned to cover a yearly dinner for *The Citizen's* society page would be an out-and-out drag for any reporter, let alone one whose passion was investigative journalism. Being sent to the annual May dinner meeting of the Ambiguity Society, however, was a bit of a coup for Bonnie Livingston, so she didn't mind the traffic she had to fight on Derry Road, or the downpour that hit while she was pulled up at a gas station.

The members of the Ambiguity Society were an incredibly strange bunch. The principal aim of the group was clearly stated in the motto that adorned its letterhead:

"Prevaricate! Obfuscate! Flummox!"

That the letterhead contained neither telephone number nor address, was, of course, entirely to be expected.

Although the abiding tenet of an Ambiguity Society member's existence was to live life without ever responding directly or communicating clearly, as individuals they were harmless enough, and they were certainly amusing to the few outsiders who had ever heard of them. But their relationship with the press, whose self-appointed guardianship of the truth was as passionate as the society's love of deception, had become a competition. To reporters, the members' evasive and misleading responses to their questions were such an irresistible red flag that they were invariably willing to wade through the most enigmatic conundrums to find even the tiniest kernel of factual information.

Bonnie's excitement stirred, therefore, as she pulled into the parking lot of the Mono Cliffs Inn. When she got out of her car, she walked right into Bruno Steubens, the society's outgoing president.

Bruno nodded without smiling. "You found us again this year, Mrs. Livingston." It was not a question, simply a greeting.

"This will be the third consecutive annual meeting of the Ambiguity Society for me, Mr. Steubens. Quite a feat you have to admit. Now, since nobody from the media has ever covered four ... ah ... you wouldn't care to tell me the date of next year's meeting, would you? So my record can continue intact?"

She hastened to add, "I've always been fair in my coverage, haven't I?"

Bruno Steubens stroked his chin slowly and nodded ever so slightly. "That you have, I suppose. Been fair, I mean."

"So," Bonnie pressed a bit harder. "It's not unreasonable to ask for next year's date is it?"

Bruno continued nodding. "I guess not. I guess not. All right, well. It's going to be like this year, in the middle of the month."

"Oh really, Bruno. You can do better than that. She's really such a nice young person. For a reporter." It was Sally Steubens. Bonnie had not seen her get out of the car. "It'll be after the thirteenth, dear," she said to Bonnie. "After the thirteenth."

"Just a minute there!" The incoming president, Karen Di Creche, suddenly appeared from the other side of the parking lot along with her husband, Julio. "Are you discussing next year's meeting? That's my territory now! Look, we'll tell you this much. Next year's meeting will be on an odd-numbered date. Now does that help you?"

"Not only on an odd-numbered date," Julio contributed, "but on a date that is not a perfect square."

"I think you're going to confuse her with that, Julio." Karen turned to Bonnie and smiled indulgently. "He does that, you know. Sometimes he's just so misleading. Now, you'll have to excuse us. The executive can't be late for dinner, can we?"

With that, the four brushed past Bonnie toward the inn. She was writing furiously, concentrating so intensely that she was unaware of Sally Steubens until she whispered in her ear.

"Before the thirteenth, okay? It's all so ambiguous dear, isn't it? You know none of us is supposed to tell you the exact truth, but I just did, so now you should have the answer." With that, Sally hurried after the others.

When will the next annual meeting be held?

Solution on page 197

29

The Case of the Missing Body

For some reason, even before she picked up the telephone, Lesley Simpson knew she wasn't going to like this call. Then, when the smarmy voice of Eddy Duane greeted her, she knew her instincts had been right on. Eddy Duane was a lawyer in the crown attorney's office. He was not on Lesley Simpson's list of favorite people.

"Hey Les! How are ya?" "Les" would have spoiled the day in any case. Lesley hated being called "Les." Her name was "Lesley," spelled with an E-Y. "The British way," her mother had explained.

"Better brace yourself, Les! We're finally gonna charge your favorite client with murder." That got Lesley's attention. "You see, Les, old kid, we found his wife's body. Well, her skeleton really. It's the late Mrs. Vincent Gene, all right. Absolutely no question. We'll need the dental records to confirm it, but there's no doubt it's her. The ring on the finger, the one earring, the clothes, the shoes. And you know where she was found? Right in the backyard! Your boy's not too bright, Les! Burying his wife in the backyard!"

Suddenly Eddy Duane's voice became more serious. "Look, Lesley," he said. "I'll meet you in, say, an hour or so out at Vincent

Gene's house. Cops are there now. The coroner, too. We've agreed to leave everything till you get to see it. One hour. Okay?"

With that, Eddy Duane hung up. Lesley realized she hadn't said a single thing on the telephone other than answering with her own name. Still, conversation wasn't necessary. Not in this case. It was three years old, but Lesley knew every detail as though it had started only yesterday.

Three years ago, the wife of gentleman-farmer Vincent Gene had left her husband sitting at the breakfast table of their expensively renovated Caledon farmhouse and was never seen again. That there had been foul play was pretty certain. Her car was found only minutes away from the house on a barely passable, unmaintained sideroad. It was full of blood – the type matched hers; the front seat had been sliced, presumably with a knife; and a single earring was found on the floor of the passenger side. But her body, if indeed she was dead, had never been found.

Vincent Gene, the husband, was Lesley Simpson's longtime client, and although he insisted he was innocent, the police had focused on him from the beginning. Only the lack of a body, Lesley knew, kept them from laying a murder charge. Now, it seemed, the last hurdle may have been cleared.

It took Lesley only forty minutes to get to Vincent Gene's farm. She noted with relief that Eddy Duane wasn't there yet. Lots of activity though – several police cars, an ambulance, a growing knot of neighbors gathering around the forsythia bushes at the end of the laneway. Near the back of the property, standing beside a back-hoe, Lesley recognized Sergeant Rodney Palmer. The recognition was mutual.

"Ah, Ms. Simpson. We've been expecting you," the sergeant said as Lesley approached. Rodney Palmer was as polite as Eddy Duane was pushy. "Over here, if you want to take a look." He took Lesley over to a narrow trench that began where the bucket of the backhoe rested on the ground and ran to a small barn some distance away. Two policemen in coveralls were standing in the trench, their heads just below the top edge.

"It's supposed to be for a water line running to the barn," Palmer said. "They've been digging here four or five days." He nodded at the backhoe. "Operator found the body – uh, the *skeleton,* rather – first thing this morning. Well, actually, he turned up a shoe first; then when he saw a bone, he stopped and called us. We've almost finished uncovering the whole skeleton now. Wasn't that difficult 'cause the clothes are still in good shape. You want to see?"

Lesley took a deep breath. Then another one. "Yes," she replied.

Rodney Palmer took a few steps and pointed down into the trench without speaking. When Lesley followed and looked down, she knew the sight would stay with her forever. Whatever she had expected, it certainly wasn't color, yet that's what she noticed most of all. Color. The green grass at the top of the trench. Trampled but still green. Then the neat, precise layer of dark brown topsoil. And under that, almost as if someone had drawn a line, a band of yellow. Sand, Lesley figured. Then below that, right to the bottom, blue clay. Maybe it was the blue, she thought, that made the clothing on the skeleton look so, well, so elegantly crimson, dirty as it was.

"See the one earring inside the skull, Les?" The sudden intrusion of Eddy Duane almost made Lesley stumble into the trench. "Quite a sight, huh? One your client never expected to see again, I'll bet. And you know what, it almost worked, too. You see the trench? It was supposed to go over there." He pointed to a spot several yards away. "But there's too much rock, so without even asking, the backhoe guy dug this way and *voilà!* The late Mrs. Vincent Gene. Right in her own backyard!"

Lesley Simpson looked straight at Eddy Duane. "Mrs. Gene," she said, "if indeed that is Mrs. Gene, was not buried here. Not when she died anyway." She shifted her gaze to Sergeant Rodney Palmer. "My guess is that if you can find out who dumped the skeleton into this trench last night and covered it up, you'll have the person who did the killing, too."

How does Lesley Simpson know that the skeleton was dumped into the trench last night?

Solution on page 198

30

The Case of the Marigold Trophy

Janice Sant bit into a fresh wedge of orange and concluded that at least one of her five senses was working normally. The other four had slid into that never-never land the body finds when it has been doing the same thing in the same place for too long.

Since five o'clock, when the Palgrave Community Library opened for its Tuesday hours, Janice had been sitting in front of a microfilm viewer, slowly winding her way through back issues of *The Daily Enterprise*. Her sense of touch had long since disappeared into the hard wooden chair on which she sat. Only her right hand, which slowly cranked the microfilm across the screen, gave assurance that she could feel anything. She knew her eyes were still working for they continued to refocus after each movement of the old-fashioned type. But whether the focusing was a conscious act or simply a reflex after hours at the screen, she couldn't be sure.

Before she could assess the two remaining senses, Eugene Weller's cologne told her that at least one of them was still working.

"I'll be closing in about five minutes, Miss Sant." The gentle, elderly librarian beamed down at her. "It's actually five past nine already."

Janice looked over the viewer at the portly little man. He was compulsively arranging the little boxes of microfilm into three separate piles: 1903, 1904 and 1905.

"How have you done?" He walked around the table and put his face very close to the screen. The cologne was even stronger now. Janice knew he must be one of those types who dab it on all day long. "Goodness!" He straightened slightly, leaving a wave of scent behind. "March 3 already! You've done quite well, haven't you? Still think you should have taken a break though. Young people like you shouldn't skip meals." He walked around to the other side of the table again and tapped one of the piles of little boxes to make it absolutely symmetrical. "Just turn off the switch when we close. I'll put things away tomorrow. Sorry again about the missing October. No one knows why that month was never filmed. Don't forget now," he said as he walked away, "five minutes."

Janice sighed and then sighed again when she tried unsuccessfully to wind the film along, for her hand had gone to sleep. What made her weariness and discomfort even worse was that this job was a freebie. Normally, she charged between $50 and $75 an hour plus expenses for an investigation, but this job she had volunteered for. On the surface it had seemed very simple. Ownership of the Palgrave Horticultural Society's proudest and by far most valuable – and beautiful – possession was being challenged. It was a trophy, a marigold, about the size of a teacup, set in a cluster of natural Baffin Island graphite on a base of local black walnut. The flower itself was twenty-four carat solid gold. On a rectangular plate set into the walnut were etched the words:

M. TOOCH
GRAND CHAMPION MARIGOLDS
ALBION AGRICULTURAL EXHIBITION
10 JULY 1904

When Miss Maribeth Tooch died in 1960, well into her nineties, her will had bequeathed this most unusual trophy – work of art, really – to the society. Unfortunately, it was tainted with an unresolved controversy. Maribeth's twin sister, Maribel, until her death in 1959, had steadfastly claimed that she had been the rightful winner and not the runner-up as the records indicated, because Maribeth had broken the rules.

Undaunted, since 1960 the Palgrave Horticultural Society had proudly displayed the Tooch trophy until two weeks ago, when its ownership was challenged in court by Rachel Tooch-Rothman, a grand-niece of Maribel, and her late husband, Denison. Janice's task, if it could be done, was to find out the truth once and for all.

So far, from *The Daily Enterprise*, she had learned that Maribeth had indeed been awarded the grand championship with Maribel coming second and that this most valuable and unusual trophy was a one-time gift of an anonymous benefactor. She had also learned that there were indeed rules for the marigold contest: requirements governing the type of seed that could be used (Stratus or Givern), specifications regarding exactly when the seeds could be sown (on February 23), instructions that the flowers had to be cut on the day before the Exhibition (on July 9), and a rule that winners were ineligible the following year. Janice had also discovered that she could wind her way through about five months of newspaper every hour, and although she had worked through the issues of *The Daily Enterprise* carefully and in sequence, she had still not found anything to help her clear up the controversy itself.

Not until Eugene Weller and his cologne had intruded to tell her it was closing time. That had woken her up, and later, she acknowledged she'd have missed it otherwise. Really, there had been no logical reason to pay attention to the story on the screen at the time.

The headline was, at best, curious and the story itself was similar to the stuff she had been skimming over with steadily decreasing attention as time wore on.

TWO TIME RUNAWAY

For the second time in only a very brief period, a horse owned by Mr. Curragh O'Malley has run away and injured a citizen. In yesterday afternoon's incident, the horse made contact with Mr. Ezra Templeton of Gibson Street while he was standing in his front yard. Mr. Templeton has suffered a broken arm. Mr. O'Malley explained that the horse was tethered in front of the Dominion Hotel while he was conducting business inside, and it was frightened by some young boys playing hoop-and-stick. On the same day a week earlier, this horse broke its tether at the same hitching rack and struck down Miss Maribeth Tooch of Pine Street. Coincidence being what it is, Miss Tooch had only just stepped outside her solarium for a few seconds of fresh air after seeding marigolds for the annual exhibition in July. It was at this precise instant that the horse ran onto her property. Miss Tooch suffered bruises but no broken bones.

Her friends and acquaintances, and those of Mr. Templeton, will be pleased to know that both of these fine citizens are recovering nicely. Nevertheless *The Enterprise* believes that tethering by-laws in Palgrave must be more rigorously enforced if innocent people are to enjoy the simple privilege of standing in their own yards.

"I'm turning the lights out, Miss Sant. Oh, Miss Sant, I'm going to turn ... Why Miss Sant! You look very upset! What's the matter?"

Eugene Weller rushed over to her in a cloud of concern and freshly applied cologne.

"Our beautiful trophy," Janice said. "We could lose it!"

?

Why does Janice Sant think the Palgrave Horticultural Society could lose its most prized possession?

Solution on page 198

31

The Coffee Break That Wasn't

"Receiving and disposal look all right," Di Froggatt said as she came back from what had started out as a simple trip to the washroom. "As a matter of fact, not bad at all for a place like this, since they've got to share space with the deli next door." Having once been a health inspector, Di couldn't resist an opportunity to check things out. "Bit messy at the loading door," she went on, "but nothing that would warrant a charge. Normal really, for a Friday morning."

As she sat down, her knee bumped the single leg in the center of the table causing Lennie Strachan's cup of coffee to sway danger-ously in its bright white plastic cup. Quickly Lennie put her spoon in the steaming brew to stop the swirling and without looking up said, "Don't apologize. I bumped it twice when you were out. There must be a special annex in hell for people who design furniture like this." She lay the spoon on the table and grinned at Di.

"Just try to sit up straight and be comfortable for more than three seconds. The seats are even worse!"

Lennie and Di were sitting – or at least were attempting to sit – in a small restaurant at the end of a shopping mall. The little restaurant was ultra modern. It's very name suggested what was expected of the clientele: Eat 'n' Run it was called. The place was exceptionally bright, almost painful to the eyes with its intense fluorescent glow, and in an antiseptic kind of way, it appeared to be squeaky clean.

To anyone who ate but failed to run immediately, it was soon obvious that the designer of the restaurant did not intend that customers should relax here. The tables were a study in flimsy molded plastic; so were the chairs. But it was their color that mounted the final assault: bright mauve with even brighter orange trim. As a result, most of the customers at Eat 'n' Run did exactly that, many of them without even realizing why. Except for, on this particular morning, Lennie Strachan and Di Froggatt.

Di took a deep breath and sighed. "Well, it sure isn't Lum's Cafe, is it?"

Lennie nodded. Di was referring to a comfy old diner, now long gone, that had stood on the site of this same shopping mall. The two friends had met regularly at Lum's Cafe years before. They had both been inspectors then with the city's Department of Health. Now retired, they got together once in a while for coffee and a chat. But there was something about getting together like this that always turned them back into inspectors again. Somehow they couldn't help it.

"Y'know, these things," Lennie said, changing the subject as she held up a tiny plastic container with the cream sealed inside, "imagine how much easier our job would have been if these had been around?"

Di smiled. "Yeah, if we had a free cup of coffee for every jug of cream we poked our noses into, we'd go into permanent caffeine surge!"

"Yes," Lennie replied, "but in one way these things have a serious drawback. Look at this." With her index finger she pushed four of the little containers one after the other. "Both of us drink it black, yet the waitress gave us two each. Had them in the pocket of her apron. I wonder how many of these get thrown out. Years ago it was hygiene. Now it's pollution."

Lennie kept on talking, but Di Froggatt wasn't listening. She was staring at Lennie's left hand as it came up to the edge of the cup of coffee. Clamped between her thumb and index finger was a fly. A *plastic* housefly!

Di was flabbergasted. "Have you still got some of those things?" Her tone indicated she didn't need an answer.

"Three more boxes at home," Lennie said without changing expression, and dumped the little black offender into her cup of coffee. It disappeared and then surfaced immediately, floating passively on top. "Never know when they'll come in handy. Ever want to get your grandchildren to leave the table? Oh Miss!" Lennie called the waitress. "Miss!"

The waitress appeared immediately.

"Miss. Look at this!" Lennie's indignation was quiet but unmistakable.

The waitress peered a little closer, saw the fly, then without a word took Lennie's cup away and disappeared with it behind the counter. She came right back and set the cup down in front of Lennie, mumbling, "Sorry," and then dug two more cream containers out of her apron pocket. "I'll tell the manager," she said.

"Yours okay?" the waitress said to Di.

Di just nodded her head. She was intent on Lennie's next move. The waitress set down another two cream containers, this time in front of Di, and then moved away to another table.

"Well," Di said, "are you going to finish the test or not?"

Lennie's nostrils flared in mock indignation. "Watch me!" With a napkin she wiped the tip of her little finger and then touched the surface of the coffee twice. She licked the finger and looked at Di.

"I'll be darned," Lennie said.

Di leaned forward. "You mean you caught them?" she said.

This time Lennie Strachan's indignation was real. "Bet on it!" she replied.

 What offense has Lennie detected at the Eat 'n' Run and how has she done it?

Solution on page 199

32

Who Shot the Clerk at Honest Orville's?

Mary Cremer leaned back out of the doorway at 26 Division to see who had called her name.

"Here! Mary! Over here!"

This time Mary recognized the voice of her sister Caroline, but in the busy pre-Christmas bustle on the sidewalk, it took a few more seconds to locate her.

"All *right!*" Mary's enthusiasm when she finally saw her was genuine. "What are *you* doing here?"

Caroline pointed to the 26 Division lobby and gave a smile of chagrin. "Kee Park," she said.

"*What!*" Mary blurted, loud enough for a few passersby to pause in the crush and stare at the two young women.

"That ... that ... *jerk!* He's done it again! What is it that makes him think we're a package just because we're sisters?"

Caroline shrugged her shoulders. She tended to be just a bit calmer than Mary.

"It's just Baxter," she said. "I don't think he can help himself. Don't sweat about it. You've only got a few more weeks. Besides, this one's really interesting! Kee Park, I mean."

"I suppose," Mary replied. "At least ... *Omigosh!*"

Both young women had forgotten they were blocking the doorway of the busiest police station in the downtown area, until two burly plainclothes types rapped on the inside of the glass simultaneously.

"Sorry," Mary said. She opened the door and slipped in quickly. Caroline came right after her.

"At least," she went back to her point, "it isn't support payments for a change, or crummy break and enter again."

"No!" Caroline was definitely excited. "Kee Park could be really big. They charged him this morning. Murder. I ..."

"He's *charged?*" Mary grabbed her sister's coat sleeve. "I thought ..."

"That's why I'm here." Caroline said. "Baxter got a call from Detective ... Detective ... let's see." She fished a piece of paper out of her coat pocket. "Blanchard! Yes, Blanchard. Didn't we deal with him once before? Kind of cute."

"*Charged?*" Mary was still absorbing the fact that her – *their* – client had been charged with murder.

She and Caroline were law students completing their one year of practicum before being admitted to the bar. Mary's time was to end in a month. Caroline was only midway through. Their firm, Baxter, Baxter, Quisling, Keele, and Wilson – only one, the second Baxter, was still alive – regularly took on a small number of legal-aid cases, all of which were with equal regularity turned over to students. "Freebies," the surviving Baxter called them, although both Mary and Caroline had been shocked when they saw the number of hours the firm billed the government for services.

Most of the cases were single parents chasing delinquent support payments or juveniles on break-and-enter charges or shoplifting. The case of Kee Park was different. Dramatically so. He had been picked up last night at a shooting in front of Honest Orville's, the biggest discount emporium in the city, perhaps even the whole country.

At first, Park was held as a material witness only, then on suspicion of manslaughter. That's when Mary came onto the case. Now things had spun ahead by one more step during the time she traveled to the police station.

She pulled Caroline over to a bench in the lobby. "You had better fill me in."

Caroline opened her coat as she sat down. "Things have moved pretty fast in the past couple of hours." She stood up with a look of discomfort on her face and took her coat off. "I thought the city was supposed to be on a tight budget. They could save some money on the heating bill in this place. Anyway. You know all about Park claiming he was out on the sidewalk, just standing there when it happened." Caroline stopped to take off her scarf and paused to concentrate on a recalcitrant knot.

"For heaven's sake, what's the rest of it?" Mary insisted.

"Okay. Sorry. And he claims he didn't even know there was a robbery going on until these two guys burst out the door, chased by the clerk."

"Dumb." Mary shook her head. "The clerk I mean. What did the guy think? Chasing two people with a gun!"

"Yeah, but dumb or smart, he's dead," Caroline replied. "And our client is charged with his murder, and it doesn't look good."

Now Mary stood up and took off her coat. "You're right about the heat. But then, right now I guess it's got to be a lot hotter for Kee Park." She pursed her lips. "I just can't buy the murder charge. There's too much circumstantial stuff."

She sat down again. "Let's review what we've got. Two guys rob Honest Orville's about 8:30 p.m."

"8:40," Caroline inserted. "There's a time fix from the patrolman across the street."

"The witness?" Mary asked. She held up her hand. "Don't answer. It had to be him. Right?"

Caroline nodded. "Confirmed, too. He was calling in at the time."

Mary continued. "And the two guys – the robbers – run out onto the street, presumably to get lost in the Christmas shopping crowds. They're chased by the clerk. When he gets to the doorway, he gets shot."

"Not quite," Caroline said. "The patrolman had modified that a bit in his report. The shooting took place well out on the sidewalk. Under that great big huge sign. You know, the one with the fifty thousand bulbs or something like that."

Mary shook her head reflectively. "Okay. On the sidewalk, then." She paused again. "Then one of the two gets away, probably with the gun because no gun is found. That hasn't changed, too, has it?"

"No. Still no gun."

"Well, that's got to help our guy, doesn't it? So at this point our patrolman's partner comes out of the doughnut shop, and the two of them stop all the traffic and run across the street and arrest Kee Park and one other guy. The other guy's Asian, too, right?"

"Yes," Mary replied. "But Kee Park's Korean. The other one is Chinese. Name's Sung something. I've got the full name in here." She tapped her briefcase.

Mary frowned. "I still don't see how they can come up with a murder charge if they don't have the gun."

"Agreed," Caroline said. "They've vacuumed out the catch basins and gone over the sewers and picked through every garbage can for blocks and there's definitely no gun, but here's what you don't know. This morning the other guy, Sung ... whatever, after holding out all night, confessed to the robbery *and* fingered Kee Park as his partner and the trigger man. His story is that he didn't even know Kee Park had a gun."

Mary got to her feet. "And our guy's story is that he was just standing there on the sidewalk when two guys – he said they were Chinese, didn't he? – burst out of the store. One of them shoots the clerk and walks away. *Walks!* Into the crowd. The next thing he knows is he's been collared and taken here to 26."

"And now," Caroline added, "charged with murder."

Mary began to pace. "I can't believe there isn't another witness. Only that patrolman."

"In that part of town?" Caroline raised one eyebrow. "You know what it's like down there. Hear no evil, see no evil." She grinned. "Speak it though. And for sure, *do* it!"

"So what does Baxter want us to do?" Mary asked, as much to herself as to her sister.

Caroline reached for her briefcase and stood up. "He's confident that getting the murder charge reduced as a first step will be pretty easy. Everything's so messy. No gun for instance. But what he wants us to do is to slow things down until we can get more time to assess what really happened. Also, to see if we can find any holes that will either reduce the charge further or maybe even blow it away. He said that once Kee Park is charged, then it becomes a case of our having to *dis*prove. It's easier if the burden of proof is on the other side."

"So we have to find reasonable doubt," Mary said.

"And the faster the better," Caroline replied.

? **Of the several elements in the case that Mary and Caroline can present to evoke "reasonable doubt," there is one that stands out just a bit. What is that one?**

Solution on page 199

33

Speed Checked by Radar

"Who's that?" Fran Singleton pointed at a young man who had come out a side door and was now walking at a measured pace through the parkette toward a little annex building nearby. "And what's that building he's going to?"

"Dunno," Aaron Gold answered. "The guy, I mean. The building – it's for duplicating. Serves the whole complex here." He leaned closer to the steering wheel to get a better look at the young man without being too obvious. "No, I dunno," he repeated. "Could be what we're lookin' for. Maybe. Bit young though, don't you think? He's probably a grunt. Sure doesn't look like a terrorist, anyway. But then neither did that little old granny who carried in the bombs at Woodbridge, did she?"

"Grunt?" Fran thought she knew, but the young constable with her loved to use words that he knew she was unsure of. Aaron Gold did everything he could to make Fran think the generation gap was a chasm.

"Yeah, *grunt*. One of those career minimum-wage types. Room temperature I.Q. Does all the donkey work. Nothing that takes any cells." He tapped his forehead. "Can't tell time at 9 a.m., but scorches the mat when it's 5 p.m. Lots of those types in there."

Fran watched the grunt – or terrorist – pause at the bottom of the steps to the windowless little building and look around, first to the left, then to the right. She saw the young man shift what appeared to be a bundle of file folders from under his right arm to under his left as he went up the steps. Then from a huge ring chained to his belt, he selected a key, and in a single motion, unlocked the door, opened it, and walked in. The gray metal slab closed automatically behind him.

"You see him look around like that?" Aaron Gold asked. "Before he went in?" When Fran didn't answer he kept on talking. "Could be checking things out. There's always duplicating to be done at this time of day, and they may have sent him out so things would seem normal. And so he could take a look, too." He paused. "Then on the other hand he could just be planning to sneak a smoke when he's in there and was just checking for supervisors. These are all non-smoking buildings now. That's hard on the grunts."

Fran didn't respond out loud; she just nodded. She was looking back at the main building again, looking for signs of anything unusual. If the building was under some kind of threat, there was nothing obvious. It was a small building by government standards, only two stories, easy to take in at a single glance. All of the windows had standard-issue vertical blinds and all of these were open, presumably to take advantage of the late afternoon sun. After a long, uncomfortable winter, this was the third day in a row of balmy spring weather.

Fran peered even harder. There was nothing unusual at all. A single fresh graffito made a cynical comment on the brass door plate that proclaimed the building to be the property of the Internal Revenue Service, Investigations Branch, but that certainly was not unusual. No, Fran could not see anything wrong at all. There was the expected amount of movement behind the blinds. Except, come to think of it, the corner offices on both floors. And the blinds on those two weren't as wide open as the others! Or was she overdoing it? Nothing says there *has* to be movement in every office, does it?

Ever since the bombing incident in Woodbridge last month, which had flattened still another I.R.S building, everybody was jumpy; the slightest suspicion was treated very seriously. Still, Fran thought, there is a limit.

"The thing is, the guy appeared normal enough, didn't he?" Aaron Gold was still speaking, and Fran realized she hadn't been paying attention. "But then they're not stupid; they're not gonna send somebody out to make things look cool and then have him draw attention to himself are they? Y'know, maybe we should ..." *Beep beep beep beep beep beep beep ...*

On the dash, the radar monitor lit up and started the incessant beeping that every officer hated with a passion. At the same time, it shut down Aaron Gold's continuing assessment of the subject's likely purpose and Fran Singleton's analysis of what was happening in the Revenue building.

"A live one! Good!" Fran began to talk fast in spite of herself. "Get out and pull him over," she instructed Aaron, "but just chew him out and then get him out of here! This has got to look normal, but no citations! I don't want you bogged down and I don't want any bodies between us and the building, so get rid of him as fast as you can."

Before she even finished, Aaron was on the street pointing a silver-gray Mercury Sable to the curb.

"Okay," Fran said, grabbing the transmitter, "if this is cover, then now we're covered."

She tapped the SEND button twice. From outside it would surely appear like a normal call-in. Possibly a check of the Mercury with a central computer.

But what she said was, "This is Command. This is Command. Stay put! Everybody stay in place! This is just a speeder. Everybody stay put."

Fran Singleton was speaking to eight heavily armed personnel in combat uniforms. They were deployed, well out of sight, around the I.R.S building but were ready to move on her signal.

About thirty minutes ago she had been sneaking a listen to the four o'clock news, waiting for the sports and the Stanley Cup commentary – the Flyers played the first of two weekend games tonight – when Sergeant Horowycz had interrupted.

"I.R.S building again, Inspector Singleton," he'd said. In their precinct that needed no elaboration.

"No response on the 4 p.m. check. Phone company says the line's okay, but we can't raise their switchboard. Probably we're all spooked by Woodbridge, but I don't like it. Thought I should tell you."

Horowycz was experienced. He didn't panic. And because he didn't like it, Fran took only about ten seconds to decide that the Emergency Response (E.R.) team was needed. She simply couldn't afford to fool around. The building was a regular for bomb threats. At income tax time they cleared the place at least every second day on average; that's why her precinct made a telephone check every hour on the hour. After the Woodbridge incident last month – two fatalities in that one – everybody was understandably on edge.

What she didn't want to do, however, was turn on the crazies, and that was her dilemma. She knew that if the E.R. team rushed the building for a false alarm, the media would have a field day and every nutcase in the city would get the idea. That's why she and

Constable Gold had set up a radar speed trap out front – a perfectly logical and, she hoped, unobtrusive way to case the place first.

In the few minutes they'd been out front, neither Fran nor Aaron had seen cause for suspicion, except maybe those two quiet offices on the corners. The only activity they'd seen was the young man going to the annex.

He came out now – burst out actually – pushing the door open with his bottom, both arms loaded with paper, and sprinted down the steps.

As he hustled back to the main building, Fran tried to convince herself that he wasn't really moving a lot faster than he had when going the other way. The young man looked out at Aaron who still had the driver of the Mercury at the curb. Although Fran studied him closely, she couldn't be sure whether the young man had a smile or a sneer on his face. In any case, the tableau of Constable Gold and the speeder didn't appear to warrant more than a glance before he disappeared back into the I.R.S building.

She reached for the transmitter. For a few seconds she held it in front of her, evaluating her choices. Then she popped the SEND button twice.

"Command here. This is Command."

She paused again, just a bit longer than usual.

"Stand down. Repeat. The order is to stand down. Everyone stay in place, but I want nobody, I repeat, *nobody* visible." She looked at her watch. It said 4:28. "In about two minutes I expect a bunch of people to leave the building ..."

Fran slumped a bit behind the steering wheel, then adjusted the radio transmitter before tapping the SEND button several times. "This is Inspector Singleton for Sergeant Horowycz. Leshie, it's ..." She looked at her watch again. "It's 4.29. At 4:35 I'm going into the I.R.S building with Constable Gold. No one else. I'm ninety-nine percent sure things are normal. Just a check. If I don't get back to you by 4:40, assume there's trouble and send in the E.R. team."

?

What has made Fran Singleton ninety-nine percent sure that things are normal in the Internal Revenue Service building?

Solution on page 200

34

Where to Send "This Stuff Here"

Before lunch on her very first day on the job, Sue Hageman realized why she was the third assistant to equipment manager Jurgen Nodl in as many months. By the end of the first week, she was not in the least surprised to learn that hers had also been the only application for the job. For the moment, however, how she got the job, or why, was not at issue.

What was at issue was that:

1. She was in the LAME Room (lost, abandoned and misplaced equipment) of Meadowbanks Stadium in Edinburgh, Scotland.

2. She was standing in the midst of a pile of items which, except for a set of skis to go to Turin, were like Iago Cassini's photography bag and had nothing whatever to do with sports, especially football.

3. She had been handed a ratty brown envelope labeled: *Dispersal – Names & Addresses* by Nodl, who had apparently taken off for parts unknown.

4. He had told her to arrange for the immediate shipment of "this stuff here," to the "names and addresses in there."

"This stuff here," she was able to figure out, with the help of the equipment manager of the Glasgow Rangers, the only other person in the LAME Room when Nodl disappeared, was the personal belongings of the Veneto Thunderbolts. Well, not quite. "This stuff here" was only *certain* personal belongings of the Veneto Thunderbolts left over after Jurgen Nodl, in a rare fit of efficient performance, had trundled the rest of it, in fact all except these four open cartons, off to the shipping dock. The four cartons, each with items belonging to four different players from four different cities, had found their way into the LAME Room and into Sue Hageman's charge.

The Thunderbolts had celebrated long and hard last night after taking a week to win a soccer tournament (Sue was still having trouble getting used to calling it "football" here at Meadowbanks). Then except for Sue, Nodl, and one assistant coach, the players had run for the airport, leaving the team administration to send on their belongings and equipment.

"You just have to get it to the right airport." The manager of the Glasgow team was very helpful, in part, because he was one of the many former employees of the Thunderbolts and felt sorry for Sue. "It's the players' responsibility from that point. Half these fellows never go straight home anyway. Now you take those chess sets there." He half-waved at a carton Sue was straddling. "Belong to that fellow from Capri, I forget his name. Now, he won't go right home. Never does. I'll bet he'll be off to play for one of the South American teams. Season starts there real soon. They're all like that. Except maybe for the center-half from Milan. He and his wife got a business there."

He pointed to the brown envelope in Sue's left hand. "Jurgen's awfully unorthodox, but strangely enough he gets the job done. They say you just have to get used to his ways. I never could though. Not very many can. Still, I'm sure the four names and locations you need'll be in there."

After that, Sue dared to look in the envelope for the first time. There was nothing that even approached a manifest or an inventory or a list of names and addresses. Instead there were scraps and bits of paper. There were personal letters, one from Tino Savi declining Nodl's invitation to go skiing. Savi said that he did not ski, and that in any case, he and Giovanni Moro would be visiting in Naples at the time. Interestingly, there was an invoice for skis and ski boots; it was marked paid but the name had been torn off. Another invoice was addressed to Mrs. Gino Bellissime in Milan, but that was it. Just name and address. What was being invoiced was not included.

Sue sighed. This was not going to be easy, but at the very least, now she knew where to send the guitar.

Where and to whom will Sue Hageman send the guitar?

Solution on page 201

A Witness in the Park

At the bottom of a little knoll, Mary Blair paused and looked back at her footprints in the frosty grass. She was grateful she'd decided to wear flats at the last minute. With high heels she would never have been able to walk on the lawn like this for the ground was not yet frozen.

Mary turned a complete 360 degrees. There was no sign of Alicia Bell yet, but that didn't surprise her. It was still too early. She shaded her eyes against the sun as it rose over the top of the knoll, shortening its shadow and shortening hers, too.

Both the public park just to her left, surrounded by an imposing if somewhat ancient iron fence, and the unfenced section of lawn where she was standing had been landscaped years ago into a series of mounds or knolls. None of them were any higher than the average adult, but they gave the impression of rolling terrain, especially from far away. In the park itself, a series of gravel paths and beds of exotic flowers wound their way around the little knolls. Someone had once explained to Mary that the park had been landscaped this way in order to force people to walk through it slowly.

Indeed there was no other park like it in the city. Even its name was impressive: Rousseau Place Botanical Observatory. And it was also unique because it didn't cost the city a cent. Rousseau Place Botanical Observatory was maintained – and very well, too – by a pair of wealthy but extremely eccentric flower growers. One of them, Jack Atkin, was Mary Blair's biggest client. The other, Ron Minaker, couldn't be for he was Jack Atkin's arch rival. It was yet another incident in the long-running feud between the two that had brought Mary to the park at a time of day when she preferred to be in bed, or at the very least, dawdling over breakfast. Mary was not an early riser.

"Here I am!" A voice disturbed Mary's reverie. "I say, Ms. Blair, good morning!" A rather stout lady in a tweed suit and an odd Victorian-looking hat was covering the closest knoll at a half trot. "You *are* Ms. Blair, the lawyer, aren't you? I hope I'm not late, am I? You did say eight o'clock. I had to walk all the way around the park because the gates are locked. They're not opened till ten."

"It's okay. It's okay. You're not late," Mary assured the newcomer. "And yes, I'm Mary Blair. If you know who I am, then you must be Alicia Bell, the witness." She shook Alicia's hand. "Thank you for coming. It's important that we go over what you saw Ron Minaker do before I initiate any formal legal action. You see, you're the only witness, and I want to get a handle on things right here at the scene of the crime so to speak." What Mary Blair did not add was that she also wanted to get a handle on Alicia Bell.

"I understand," Alicia replied. "I've been involved in this kind of thing before. As a witness, I mean. For Mr. Atkin, too, about ten years ago. It was the time that Mr. Atkin and Mr. Minaker got into that dispute over who had developed a blue azalea."

Mary's eyebrows went up at that one. It had been before her time. She had become Jack Atkin's lawyer five years ago, and in the period since, Atkin had sued Minaker – or vice versa – no less than six times. Every single one of the cases had been thrown out by the trial judge, who then proceeded to scold the two adversaries. And their lawyers! Mary was trying to avoid a repeat embarrassment, which was one of the reasons she had asked Alicia Bell to meet here.

"Now tell me one more time," Mary said, "what it is you saw Mr. Minaker do."

Alicia Bell cleared her throat. "It's quite simple really. As you know, inside the park there are twenty-six flower beds. Mr. Atkin has thirteen. Mr. Minaker has thirteen. The bed over in the far southeast corner is Mr. Atkin's. Has been since they took over the park. Two days ago, in the morning, I saw Mr. Minaker on his knees in that bed. He had a little shovel and he was digging flower bulbs. Digging them *out*, and putting them in a garbage bag."

Mary Blair's voice dropped a few tones as she slid into her cross-examination mode. "You're absolutely sure which flower bed it was?"

"Oh indeed!" was Alicia's reply, "the one in the southeast corner for sure. No doubt about that."

Mary pushed a little harder. "But surely Mr. Minaker saw you, and he wouldn't dig the bulbs out if he knew you were watching."

"Ah, but he couldn't see me!" Alicia Bell's eyes lit up. "Well, he *could* have, I suppose, if he tried real hard. But he didn't. You see, he didn't know I was there. I was behind the knoll in back of the flower bed, something like you and I are right now."

Mary pounced on that one. "But if you're behind one of these knolls," she said, "you can't see what's on the other side!"

Alicia Bell was waiting for it. "Of course not. But I wasn't all the way down at the bottom. More like halfway." She pulled at Mary's elbow and led her up the knoll a few steps. "See? Look! Here we are, only halfway up and you can see *everything* on the other side. They're only little mounds, these things."

Mary nodded but didn't say anything. She had to admit that it was really quite easy to be concealed and still see everything on the other side.

"If you doubt me," Alicia went on, "just wait until we can get into the park, and I'll show you precisely where I was standing. It was a day just like this. Sunny, but a real nip in the air. Leaves falling." She pointed to the frosty grass. "And you could see your tracks in the lawn just like ours here."

Mary nodded again, and again she didn't say anything. But she had heard enough. She was glad she'd got up so early, for she was convinced now that Alicia Bell was a professional witness. A witness available to the highest bidder.

 What has led Mary Blair to this conviction?

Solution on page 202

An Urgent Security Matter at the U.N.

It had always been Chris Fogolin's personal conviction that problems come in series of three. His brother Paul insisted that when you worked at the U.N. building, it was never quite that simple. Paul maintained that if diplomats were involved, there was always sure to be a fourth problem, which, given time, would turn out to be not the fourth, but the first of a new series of three. In the past half hour, the two brothers were already up to five problems and counting.

Chris and Paul Fogolin were members of the security branch at the U.N. building in New York. (Paul had once argued that just being in New York and working for the U.N. counted as problems one and two all by themselves!) At 8:45 a.m. their director had given them hands-on responsibility for a meeting to be held in the Singapore Room on the 22nd floor, at ten o'clock. The security level was "Red AA." For the Fogolin brothers that meant problem number one, for Red Double A signified a situation involving antagonists. Usually, this meant diplomats from countries at war or about to go to war or just finished with a war. It was not at all unusual to have all three conditions at once.

The second and third problems were making the room entirely secure and establishing an entrance/exit-pass system. Normally this would not be difficult, for there were procedures for both situations. But Chris and Paul had only an hour and fifteen minutes to activate them.

The fourth problem – or the first in a new series of three – was the seating arrangement. Diplomats sparring with each other over political issues often spent days, sometimes weeks, fighting furiously about protocol. One of the most intense, not to mention tedious and sustainable battles at a U.N. meeting was over just who would sit where. Fortunately for the Fogolin brothers, the chair of the meeting in this case was Ambassador Manamoto of Japan. Not only was he a neutral party in this conflict, he was a diplomat of long experience and a popular choice as chair because of his reputation for being utterly impartial. One of his unvarying conditions was that during face-to-face meetings between antagonistic parties, the delegations had to be intermingled.

He was also very astute. Manamoto had already sent Paul to replace the rectangular table in the Singapore Room with a large round table so there would be no dispute over who sat at the head or the foot. Then he sent both brothers to canvass the six participating diplomats in order to learn their seating preferences in advance.

"The vice-chair will be Mr. Bjarni Benediktsson, the attaché from Iceland," Manamoto had said to them just before they left. "Now I'm sure he will have no particular seating preference, but it would be an act of courtesy to consult him."

Even though the Fogolins thought there was no time for it, they knew all about the crucial importance of diplomatic courtesy, so they went immediately to the office of the attaché from Iceland. As it turned out, it was from him that they learned the problem count had gone up to five.

"I cannot verify this," Benediktsson intoned, "and I surely don't have to tell two such as you about the way rumors ricochet about this building. Nevertheless," he cleared his throat, "the information I have, the source of which, naturally, I cannot reveal, is of sufficient force and credibility that you should neither discard nor discount it."

Paul chanced a sidelong glance at his brother. The two of them never failed to be impressed by the fact that the quality of English they heard in this building, from people who had had to learn the language, was always so much better than what they ever heard on the streets of New York.

"My information is that there may be an assassin among the delegates at the table today. Of course I don't know who it is, or I would tell you. However, I can tell you that based on my involvement in, and knowledge of, the conflict being discussed here today, it is my ... my ... my *gut feeling,*" Benediktsson cleared his throat and made a face, "that the intended victim is Bishop Leoni, if only because he is a most vociferous exponent of his cause and certainly, as a result, has the most visible profile of anyone on that negotiating team. Even more than General Nardone."

Chris raced back to Ambassador Manamoto with that information while Paul went off to Bishop Leoni's office. Manamoto expressed mild surprise, mostly at the thought that he had not heard the rumor by now, but agreed that if it were true, Bishop Leoni was certainly a likely target. Before Chris was able to suggest a postponement, however, the ambassador went on to say that if meetings at the U.N. were canceled every time such a rumor floated to the surface, absolutely nothing would get done in the place.

"Just get on with the task, young man," he said, ushering Chris into the hall. "Ten a.m. As planned and scheduled." He placed his right palm over the back of his left hand and held them in front of his chest. "This does indeed make the seating arrangements more important, as I'm sure you realize?"

With that, Chris double-timed it down the hall to the elevators. There were six diplomats to speak to in – he looked at his watch – fifty-five minutes! Luckily, his first stop was productive. Dr. Perez was not in her office, but her secretary, a frowsy gum chewer in a sweater that was way too tight, told him in classic in-your-face Bronx style that "If Dr. Perez has to sit beside that Gestido witch from the other side, she walks. Is that clear?"

Chris was almost out the door before she could shift the wad of gum around to add, "And she won't sit beside Leoni. Or her creep boss, Nardone, either. They're grabbers!"

Chris turned and ran, as much to get away from the gum as to find Paul, but first he had to stop at Ambassador Haruna's suite. Haruna was head of his delegation and had a reputation for arrogance that was fully sustained when Chris was ushered to his desk. Without even looking up, Haruna motioned "just stand there" with his index finger and then continued to read the front section of *The New York Times*.

He still hadn't looked up or even acknowledged Chris's presence when he started to speak. "As head of the delegation I expect to be seated next to the chairperson, naturally. And I would like to arrange that ..." A door in the wall to Chris's left opened, and the ambassador looked up for the first time, an expression of extreme annoyance on his face. It stayed that way while an aide tiptoed to the edge of the desk, turned the intercom to OFF and then disappeared as quickly as possible through the same door. The silence continued for a few more long seconds.

"I understand the table will be a round one. Very well. I would like one of my delegation directly beside me – Ms. Gestido. That should be no problem for you? She's essential to me for translation.

You know what happens to General Nardone's English when he gets excited. Now, of course she won't want to sit beside the bishop, so I expect you to take care of that, too."

The ambassador had looked up at Chris only briefly. He was concentrating now on preparing a large Cuban cigar. "I trust you have been told by my aides that I have a need for ample supplies of fresh water because of some medication I am taking." Chris hadn't been told, but he had no intention of getting an aide in trouble by saying so. "So I would appreciate it if you would see to that. Those are all our requirements. You may seat our new delegate, Mr. Cresawana, wherever you wish. One must cooperate in these affairs, after all." Haruna looked up again and delivered Chris an entirely insincere smile. "I imagine you have already had enough instructions from Dr. Perez to keep you busy, haven't you?"

With that, Haruna returned abruptly to *The Times*, and in seconds, Chris was moving down the hall as fast as decorum would permit. Paul was coming from the opposite direction at the same pace.

"I can't find the bishop anywhere," Paul said as soon as they were close enough to talk. "His staff says he'll be at the Singapore Room all right, but they don't know where he is. Nardone was in though."

"Anything unusual?" Chris asked.

"Strangely, no." Paul replied. "I really thought he'd want something awkward, maybe to take Leoni down a peg – you'd almost think Leoni and not Nardone was the head of the delegation – but no, he had nothing. So are we set?"

"Well, yeah," Chris said. "We're not only set, we're being set *up!*"

"What do you mean?"

"You know your theory about the fourth problem being the first of a new series of three? Well, it's right. We've got problem number six now!"

"I don't get it."

"Wait till I tell you about the seating arrangement that Haruna wants. It's manipulation, plain and simple. He's got everybody sitting exactly where he wants them. I don't know why or what for, but he's done it. Have we got time to check the security clearance of that Cresawana guy?"

Chris turned and watched as an aide bustled past them down the hall. "Who knows?" he went on. "Maybe Benediktsson's assassination rumor is true."

?

How has Ambassador Haruna manipulated the seating arrangement? And why does Chris want to check the security clearance for delegate Cresawana?

Solution on page 203

? Solutions

1   A Decision at Rattlesnake Point
What has finally convinced Trevor Hawkes that this is a murder case?

Without doubt, Perry Provato will examine the body at the morgue, looking for possible causes of death other than trauma from the two-hundred-foot drop. Trevor, however, has drawn some preliminary conclusions because of the size of the dead person and the position of the steering column.

From Perry, and from Trevor's observation, it is clear that the dead person is big. Most particularly, he has a very big belly. If he had driven the Lincoln Town Car to the edge of Rattlesnake Point, parked it, and then jumped over in an apparent suicide, he would surely have tilted up the steering column and wheel in order to get out of the car. This is automatic behavior in large people whose cars have this feature (as all newer model luxury cars do). The fact that Trevor had to tilt up the steering column in order to get his own large frame in to peer under the seat suggests to him that someone else drove the car to Rattlesnake Point. That can only mean the victim was already dead when the car was parked there, or that he was thrown over the cliff.

This conclusion may or may not be strengthened when Ashlynne checks the pre-set radio stations. The owner surely prefers country music. If when she turns the radio on, it is not tuned to a country station, that would reinforce the contention that the driver was someone other than the owner. If the pre-set stations do not include country music stations, this may suggest further discrepancy.

Why the car was parked so carefully and locked is an issue. However, the open trunk revealed the neatness with which the vehicle was kept, likely a characteristic of the victim. It is probable that Trevor's investigation of "A." will reveal that he was an orderly person. The murderer, no doubt aware of that, must have deliberately parked and locked the car in the way that A. would have done.

2   Something Suspicious in the Harbor
What has led Sue Meisner to the conclusion that something crooked is going on aboard *The Christopher Thomas*?

On this second trip to the big freighter, Sue was able to see from her rowboat the paint scrape, where that morning the police boat had bumped into the side. Yet *The Christopher Thomas* had been receiving heavy cargo for several hours before the first visit, it was being loaded all day, and it was still being loaded when she made her unofficial trip. A freighter receiving cargo like this settles into the water as it is being loaded. Therefore, Sue should not have been able to see the paint scrape from the morning visit. By now, it should have been under water. Tomorrow morning she is going to have a careful look at the cargo, probably to see whether it is really automobile engines, or maybe to see if there is any cargo at all.

3   In Search of Answers

Why is Celeste Wyman certain that Virgil Powys was out of the studio for longer than the time he claimed to be?

It is understandable that Celeste would be suspicious of Virgil Powys. After all, he has been having difficulties with his freelance business, so a cleverly arranged theft might make it possible for him to garner two or even more fees for Hygiolic's medical discovery. But Celeste needs more than suspicion; she needs good grounds for suspecting that Powys intended to be out of the studio longer than the ten or eleven minutes he claims.

Her suspicions arise out of what she observed on the reproduction Chippendale table. The weather has been very hot so all the windows are wide open. Even though Powys's studio has windows on three walls and is on the second floor (or is, at least, elevated), there is still no movement of air for there is no breeze.

Why, then, would someone who intends to be out for only about five or six minutes (he didn't know he was going to get a phone call – or did he?) place a heavy metal stapler on his working papers unless he expected that they might be blown around? And they would be blown around only if a wind were to rise. Given the conditions at the time Powys left the studio, this was not going to be an immediate possibility; or at least not a possibility in five or six minutes. Powys apparently intended to be out of the studio for longer than he claimed, which, in Celeste's opinion, is worth probing further.

4   A Single Shot in the Chest

What does Brian Breton mean? What's wrong with the guard's story?

Brian Breton turned down an opportunity to use what were supposedly Manotik's binoculars to have a look at the ten o'clock aerobics class. His probable reason was that he did not share Roly Coyne's idea of what constitutes a good time. But what he told Roly was that he couldn't really use the binoculars because they did not have the little rubber cups on the eyepieces that are needed for people who wear glasses.

Even though there are no eyeglasses in the collection of evidence and personal effects on the table up in Roly's office, Brian realizes that Xavier Manotik wore glasses, and had for a long time, because of the callused indentations on either side of the bridge of his nose.

These two facts indicate that Manotik was not looking through binoculars at the Nucleonics executive suites. At least not *those* binoculars. Obviously Brian wonders what else in the guard's account does not hang together.

5   The Case of the Stolen Stamp Collection
Why is Mika Fleck suspicious of Miles Bender?
Miles Bender described one of the "police officers" as having blue eyes and a reddish mustache. He also said the officers had real uniforms and genuinely appeared to be motorcycle police personnel, complete with the sunglasses they typically wear. But if they had sunglasses on, how would Miles Bender have known the eye color of the one who got close to him?

6   Not Your Average Hardware Store
Gordon Pape has been to Wilfrid Norman's store before, and might recognize the hardware man, but how does Hugh Furneaux know that the dead man is not Wilfrid Norman?
In a hardware store where customers can buy "real" hardware from bins and barrels and shelves, where things are not pre-packaged in a cosmetic sort of way, the clerks get dirty hands, for obvious reasons. Over time, the hands naturally become somewhat marked by years of digging into barrels of oil-covered nails and shelves of greasy bolts. This victim had a soft, white hand showing in the small of his

back. Therefore, it surely is not Wilfrid Norman, a long-time hardware store owner.

7   Murder at 249 Hanover Street
What is Janet Dexel's reason for suspecting the butler rather than the daughter or handyman?

The butler is the only one with a careless alibi. He said he went to his
sister's in Kennebunkport on the 30th for two days. Even though his
sister may prevaricate on his behalf, he has still made the mistake of
saying the "30th." The day is October 1 (as the radio announcer
said), so if he was in Kennebunkport for two days, he could not have
gone there on September 30. There are only thirty days in September.

8   Head-on in the Middle of the Road
What is the important point that the township side has failed to bring up?

Dust. Road dust from what must be an unpaved surface (or else why
would a grader be used, and why would the rutting and potholing
recur just about every year?). The accident happened at midday on
August 9. In August, at midday, after the weather has been so nice
and dry (according to Peter Hesch's testimony), and after a road has
been repaired and graded, any car going along it will throw billows
of dust into the air. The two plaintiffs would have had to be
extremely inattentive – and therefore dangerous drivers – not to
have noticed each other's dust, blind hill or not, and so to have
been unaware of oncoming traffic.

9   A 911 Call from Whitby Towers
What is the "big hole" to which Bev Ashby refers?

Sandford Verity said that he looked up when he arrived at Whitby
Towers to see if Mr. Seneca was watching the incident out on the
street. That's when Verity allegedly saw him on the chair, which

implies he was about to attempt to hang himself with a nylon rope. However, when Bev Ashby noticed the end of a piece of nylon rope and followed the rope to where it was clamped between the balcony doors, she had to part the drapes with her pen to do so. From the street, Verity could not have seen through the drapes.

10 The Case of the Kramer Collection

What is wrong in the Kramer Collection that has left George Fewster so disappointed?

Issue number one of *Reader's Digest* is dated February 1922, so that part of the Kramer Collection may be authentic. The *Times* was begun in 1785, so the collection could quite easily have an 1890 edition. The 1728 edition of the *Saturday Evening Post* may indeed be a "genuine fraud." The magazine began publishing in 1821. In 1899, the publishers fabricated the claim that it had actually been started in 1728 by Ben Franklin. Even after the claim was proved patently false, it was never fully abandoned.

The Arctic items are quite possibly genuine for the explorers mentioned did sally forth in the years given. (And the practice of storing food in cans was developed in England for the Royal Navy in 1810, so the can of beans is okay.) The Canadian – later American – explorer Stefansson stirred up an international controversy after his "discovery" in 1910 of a group of native people on Victoria Island with fair, European features by theorizing that they had intermingled with Scandinavian colonizers years before. Stefansson called them "blond Eskimos." Thus it could be that the material in the Kramer Collection is authentic. However, it is for the coins that George is needed, and if one of them is clearly fraudulent, it's quite possible that everything else is, too.

The George Washington coins are surely legitimate. Coins were still being issued with the label *Upper Canada* well after Upper Canada became the Province of Ontario in 1867, so a half-penny dated 1883 and designated "Upper Canada" is real enough. In World War II, nickels without nickel were issued so that the valuable mineral could be used in the war effort. Coins from Hadrian's reign are common enough. But no coin produced in the B.C. era was ever labeled *B.C.* The notion of B.C. did not come into being until well after Christ was born.

11   Waiting Out the Rain
Why is Michelle Link sure that what Julie Varughese has described was not an accident?
While Michelle sat at Kline's Soda Shoppe with her friends from Memorial Junior School, she watched a little boy standing in the gutter, enjoying the rainfall. He had boots on and the runoff was rushing up against the toes of the boots. This is confirmed by the candy wrapper which flowed up to his toes and then floated between the boots. The flow of the water therefore defines the slope of the street.

Behind the little boy (and downstream) is a woman, quite likely his mother. She is standing at Whippany Appliances, next door to Kline's, listening to the news about the D-Day landing in France.

When Michelle and Julie leave Kline's, they walk past Whippany Appliances and see the two men unloading a truck belonging to Bitnik's Delivery Service. The truck is still further "downstream" from Kline's. If its emergency brake failed, it would not have rolled toward Kline's Soda Shoppe, but the other way. To cause the damage it did, the truck would have had to smash into Kline's window while under power. It was obviously not an accident.

12   A Routine Check in the Parking Lot
How does Ron Forrester know that at least one and probably both of the victims have been murdered?
The victims have been arranged in the car as though they were

lovers in a tryst. Because it is December, the motor is running to make the heater operative, and to a casual investigator that would suggest that they were overcome by carbon monoxide gas.

However, Ron notes the face of the male victim. The eyes are wide open, and most important, the pupils are very small. If the male victim had been sitting in the dark car with the lady for long enough for carbon monoxide to do its deadly work, his eyes would have adjusted to the darkness and his pupils would have been large.

Ron Forrester concludes, probably correctly, that the man was murdered elsewhere (in bright light) and then put in the car afterward. He concludes that if the man died that way, the lady probably did, too. It would have been easy to attribute their deaths to accidental carbon monoxide poisoning if he had not noticed this detail.

13　An Answer for Kirby's Important New Client

How has the Silverberg family found the answer for Kirby's client? In what year was Simon Fitzwall born?

Simon Fitzwall was born in 1789.

Ambrose Fitzwall lost his leg and three fingers two months after the Seven Years War began. Since the war ended with the Treaty of Paris in 1763, he therefore lost the leg in 1756. Smythe-Boliver was 48 then (born in 1708) and Fitzwall was half his age, or 24. Fitzwall had a daughter (Abigail, according to his personal history) who, Smythe-Boliver says, was born when Fitzwall was 18, making her 6 years old in 1756.

Fitzwall came to Halifax, and then Boston, with Abigail and Ethan and Nattie's child Rachel in 1768. (The *Earl of Shannon*, on which they sailed, sank in Halifax five years after the Treaty of Paris in 1763, under the terms of which she became a British ship.)

At the time of the crossing, Abigail would have been 18 years old. She married four years later (at the age of 22) and had a first child two years after that.

At the time of the crossing in 1768, Ethan was 3 years old (half the age Abigail was when Ambrose lost the leg) and Rachel was twice that, or 6 years old. Both Rachel and Ethan married at the same age Abigail married (22). Thus Rachel married in 1784 and Ethan in 1787. And both, like Abigail, had their first-born two years after that. Simon was Ethan's first-born in 1789.

14   Two Shots Were Fired
What is the flaw in the security guard's story that Vince Pogor is referring to?

Because of the heat wave, it is reasonable to believe that the door was indeed propped open as the guard said. And it may well be that the guard faced the front if that's where previous break-ins occurred. Therefore, his back would have been to the open door. However, even though the open door faced east, and what would therefore have been the rising sun, the fact is there was no rising sun at the time of the shooting. The area was covered with gray cloud when the shooting took place, between 6 a.m. and 7 a.m. (When Vince Pogor arrived, it was noon and the crime was already six hours old.) The sun did not come out until Vince was driving to Toronto, some time after he was about to listen to the eight o'clock news while eating his breakfast.

Given these conditions, the security guard's statement that he was startled by a dark *shadow* from the doorway behind him is highly suspect.

15   Northern Farms Ltd. Versus Dominion Spraying Company
What is the "fuzziness" Judge Mary-Joan Westlake is referring to?

Quite possibly Judge Westlake is bothered by the fact that not one of the witnesses has said, specifically and unequivocally, that he or she saw Molly's Arch Dream III in the field in question around the time that the spraying took place. Fenton Purge was not there at the time. Daphne Organ, although she is specific about having seen Molly *prior* to June 27 from time to time, says she did not pay particular attention on that morning. Eulalia Bean and Parthenon Andreikos are evasive. Their answers only imply that the cow was there at the time.

In combination, the answers become even fuzzier. Fenton Purge tells us the field is in the southwest corner of the farm. Daphne Organ, who lives right across the road from the farm, watches the sunrise from her porch while having tea (and then has lunch there because it is in the shade). Thus Daphne must face east. Regional Road 7, then, one of the borders of Farm Number 3, runs north-south. Since Parthenon Andreikos first waved to Eulalia Bean then, a few seconds later, saw the herd as he went toward the canal (south), the barn from which Eulie exits with hay is north of the field.

Eulie takes hay to a feed trough at the fence. Beside it is a water trough to which water is piped. Logically, the troughs are going to be at the fence nearest the barn.

Andreikos says the ends of the troughs pointed to the road. Therefore, the troughs were set up at the north end of this square field, perpendicular to the road. If he saw Molly broadside at her spot at the end of the trough, as he implies (having noted the triangle), then Molly would have to be facing north. The problem with his testimony is that he says the triangle was on her right side. If she was facing north, waiting for Eulie to arrive with the hay, Molly's right side would have been facing away from Road 7. Andreikos may have been able to see her broadside all right, but not the side that has the triangle. Judge Westlake has figured this out and probably wants to find out if this valuable animal might have died of hardware disease prior to or around the same time that the spraying took place. It could be that Northern Farms is simply taking advantage of a coincidence.

16   An Unlikely Place to Die
Why does Brad Matchett think that Mme de Bouvère did not die at the gazebo?

The time of day is early morning because Brad got trapped in rush-hour traffic. The gardener discovered Mme de Bouvère's body just after sunrise and turned on the alarm. The coroner estimates the time of death at between ten and eleven the night before. Therefore, if Mme de Bouvère and the man lying outside the gazebo had gone out to play tennis and indulge in some drugs the evening before, they would have walked over the lawn that surrounded the gazebo while it was still wet or at least damp from the rain that accompanied the late afternoon thunderstorm the day before. Because the gardener cuts the lawn every second day, and because he cut it yesterday, *before* they walked to the gazebo, Mme de Bouvère would surely have picked up a blade of grass (likely several) on her white sneakers. Yet Brad noticed that her sneakers, like the rest of her clothing, were pristine: entirely free of any specks. It appears to him that she somehow got to the gazebo without making contact with the lawn. Whether or not she died of a drug overdose, it is likely that someone carried her there after she was already dead.

17   To Catch a Mannerly Thief
Why is Agnes Skeehan so sure of that?

Agnes Skeehan walks into her hotel leaning into a strong east wind. She responds to Deputy Commissioner Mowat's phone call and he tells her to go right to the office of the Liverpool CID, specifically to Superintendent Opilis. Through the window of the superintendent's office, Agnes notices a weathervane on a pub across the street pointing right at her. Since the wind is from the east (blowing *toward* the west) the superintendent's office must therefore be on the east side of a street that runs north-south.

Both Agnes and the superintendent then see Alistair Withenshawe across the street, walking to the police station because he was summoned there. Opilis told Agnes that Withenshawe Purveyors has an office just a short walk to the south. Therefore, this "dude" as Agnes called him, is walking toward the north, on the west side of the street. His cane must be in his street-side hand, or *right* hand, for he first bounces it off the curb, then twirls it over parked cars.

Agnes concludes that to engage in such adept cane work, Alistair Withenshawe must be using his preferred hand, his right hand, the same hand he would use to write notes. Since the jewel thief's notes are written by a left-handed person, Agnes is willing to give odds that Withenshawe didn't write them.

18   Tracing the Couriers from Departure to Arrival
How has Mary Clare McInerney figured out where each courier is going and where each is flying from?

Mary Clare McInerney and her investigating team need to find out from which airports the drug couriers code named – or *possibly* code named – Seamus, Rothsay, Saint and Felipe are flying out, and their respective destinations as well.

The team has put together the facts that the couriers are leaving from Dorval airport in Montreal, Orly airport in Paris, O'Hare airport in Chicago, and Heathrow airport in London. The destinations that the team have discovered are Brazil (Rio), Bermuda, Hawaii (Oahu), and Hong Kong. The problem is to put the information together so that it can be determined who is flying where, and from where, so that they can be followed and the appropriate arrests made.

From Struan Ritchie, Mary Clare first learns that Rothsay is flying out of Dorval airport in Montreal, and that Seamus is going to Brazil.

Cecile King reveals that the one flying to Bermuda is flying out of Orly in Paris. That cannot be Seamus then, since he is going to Brazil. And Rothsay cannot be going to Bermuda, because she is flying out of Dorval.

When Struan calls back he reveals that Felipe is flying out of Heathrow, which means he, too, is not going to Bermuda. When Struan says that Felipe is not going to Hong Kong, it is apparent that Felipe must be the one going to Hawaii. Rothsay, then, is going to Hong Kong. The courier code named Saint must be the one going to Bermuda.

Once the team works out where the couriers are going, it is fairly easy to work out where they are flying from. They already know that Felipe is at Heathrow and Rothsay is leaving from Dorval. Saint (the one destined for Bermuda) is leaving from Orly, so Seamus must be going to Brazil from O'Hare.

19   Not All Lottery Winners Are Lucky
What has led Captain Frank Ricketts to suspect the two daughters of Archie Deschamps-Lebeau of murder?

Two days before Frank Ricketts visited the body of Archie Deschamps-Lebeau there had been a chinook. In the morning rush hour, the snow had melted to slush, and then before noon the temperature had dropped to way below freezing and stayed that way. On that day, the two daughters had supposedly visited Archie and made him lunch – this is *after* the quick thaw then freeze – and reported that he was okay. They say they found him today when they came on their regular call.

However, Archie's body had been impressed into the ice. Frank wanted to know whether Nick and the crew had measured the distance between the indentations made by his feet. He also noted that the paramedics had pried the body loose carefully and rolled him over onto his back. Frank has concluded that Archie's body was out there *before* the chinook of two days ago. (It had lain on the ice, then sank into it during the thaw, and then was frozen in when the temperature plunged.) Yet according to the daughters, the old man was all right during their visit two days ago.

20   Spy Versus Spy

What has Hauptmann Ernst August discovered? How are Kopenick and Traugott Waechter communicating in Morse code?

Because the *Rote Kapelle* did not use radios in Stuttgart to any great extent (at least in our story), the counterespionage service of German intelligence did not have great success with the direction-finding equipment used to locate clandestine radios – and thereby spies – in World War II. It is reasonable to assume, therefore, that Kopenick is not sending Morse code messages to Traugott Waechter by means of special equipment they have had installed in their vehicles. (Besides, Waechter shows up in a variety of vehicles; that would have been too much of a technical challenge had they been using such equipment.)

For obvious reasons, they would not be communicating with written signs or hand signals, not in the midst of traffic in a German city in the middle of World War II.

Then there's the fact that Hauptmann August can read the code while he is *behind* Waechter's little truck and cannot see Kopenick at all. The only way that the Morse can be used, therefore, is through the brake lights. When the vehicle stops (Kopenick's) he taps out the code to Waechter right behind him. Ernst August told Oberst Staat they had to see the two spies rendezvous while it was still raining. Either by luck or persistence, August had no doubt learned that by driving behind Waechter when the pavement was wet, he could see the brake lights of the car in front (Kopenick's) reflected off the pavement beneath the following vehicle (Waechter's). By that means August could see and translate the Morse message.

This apparently naive method of communication (Ernst August called it "clumsy") was actually used from time to time, especially in World War II. It is highly likely that real spies would not have communicated in open Morse, however, but would have had a code developed for the purpose.

The use of Morse code had declined dramatically by World War II in favor of the far more economical Baudot Code devised by a French engineer (named Baudot, what else!) in 1874. Still, who has ever heard of Baudot Code?

The *Rote Kapelle* was exceptionally successful as a Soviet network in the early years of the war, but careless use of their radios, along with increasing sophistication in radio location techniques and technology on the part of German intelligence, reduced their effectiveness by 1943. Post-war analysis, incidentally, attributes the network's downfall largely to the fact that too many agents knew one another. They did not use "cutouts" sufficiently or effectively so that when one was caught, the domino effect was very damaging.

21   The Search for Olie Jorgensson

Why does Connie Mount believe that Willy Stefan has something to tell her?

Willy Stefan, as Connie knew, is not a neutral party in this case, being Olie's uncle, Svena's brother-in-law, and perhaps most important, being married to the sister of Olie's father.

Willy has been leading the search team down the abandoned railway line at a very slow pace. He explained to Connie that the slowness was owing to the fact that signs along the trail were hard to read, there being so many tourists hiking down the line at this time of year. His mistake was in giving that as his excuse. If there were enough tourists walking along this line to disrupt the tracking process, those same hikers would have cleaned out the wild raspberries, too. Yet they grew in abundance at the edge of the trail. For reasons that Connie wants to uncover, Willy has lied to her.

22   Murder at the David Winkler House
Why does Chris Beadle believe that Kate Mistoe and Sandy Sanchez are lying? Why does she want to find out what Sandy Sanchez knows about propane systems? And how can she check out Karl Schloss's story?

Chris Beadle walked into the tiny washroom pushing the door open wide. The door barely cleared the sink in the corner ahead and to the left. The sampler is hanging on the wall behind this door. If Kate Mistoe had been nailing up this sampler when the shots were fired, she would have had to close the door. Otherwise she would not have been able to get at the wall.

The problem with her alibi arises out of the fact that Sandy Sanchez says he saw her as he passed, at the time the shots were fired. (They stared at each other in shock and fear.) If the door had been closed, he obviously would not have seen her.

When Sandy spoke to Chris and animatedly made clockwise motions with his fist to describe the tightening of the fitting on the propane system, he may have been inadvertently revealing ignorance about propane systems. Threaded fittings throughout the world are tightened clockwise and loosened counterclockwise. By international agreement, threaded fittings used in gas systems (e.g., propane) are tightened and loosened in the opposite way.

Karl Schloss had the oil changed in his car. The service station would have noted the odometer reading at the time of this oil change. By checking the odometer reading right now, Chris can calculate how far he drove after leaving the service station. By having him retrace the route he said he covered on the way back to Winkler House, Chris would be able to verify whether or not he actually did so.

23 Incident on the Picket Line

What is the attempt at fraud that Eileen Cook refers to?

You don't need to be a trucking expert to know that Roger Monk is claiming an incorrect number of tires. The police confirm that all his tires were slashed, but no tractor-trailer combination has sixteen tires.

Casual observation as you drive along the highway confirms that on the very front axle of the tractor portion of a tractor-trailer, there are two tires, one at each end. On all other axles, whether they be tandem or single or center air-lift (the type you often see retracted up off the road surface), there are always four tires, two at each end.

A little bit of logic added to this observation tells you that the least number of tires possible on a tractor-trailer combination is ten. The next largest tractor-trailer has fourteen, then eighteen, twenty-two, twenty-six, and so on. Never sixteen.

In Roger's case, he is trying for two extra tires. His tractor has a tandem axle on the rear. "Tandem" means "one behind the other." That means a total of two axles at the rear then, each with four tires (making eight), which along with the two on the very front makes ten tires on the tractor. A single axle on the trailer adds four more tires, which makes a grand total of fourteen.

24 Footprints on the Trail

Why is Inspector Torrey Mazer so certain that the footprints have been made by the suspect, Tibor Nish?

Tibor Nish does not deny using the path to get to the barn. And there is a witness who saw him there. But Nish said he came *four* days ago, which is two days before the fire. The witness thinks he came on the *day before* the fire but cannot be absolutely sure.

Then there is the matter of Tibor Nish's long legs versus the fact that the footprints are close together, implying a short-legged person. On the day before the fire, there was a thaw, a day and night of mild weather. Anyone walking down a steep hill on frozen ground, during a thaw, would necessarily take short steps, with special care to dig in the heel as much as possible to keep from falling. This is because the top few inches of earth in these conditions melts and becomes soft. This layer of soft mud on top of the frozen ground makes the surface impossibly slippery. Anyone walking on it has to be very careful and must take short deliberate steps, especially on a hill. Since the only tracks on the path are from size twelve Kodiak work boots, and since Tibor Nish does not deny using the path, the only day on which those tracks could have been imprinted was on the day before the fire: the day on which the witness thinks she saw him at the barn.

25   A Very Brief Non-Interview
What has led Sheila Lacroix to this conclusion?
When Sheila Lacroix entered the office, the office door was behind her, and the wall to her left held books and newspapers. Ahead of her (the third wall) was glass through which she could see central Amman. On the remaining wall, Ibrahim Jamaa, or rather, his substitute, was signing documents.

He had his back to Sheila and he was covered with *thobe* and *aba* so that only one hand was exposed. Since the hand rested on the back of his hip and the index finger pointed to the windowed wall, the hand therefore must have been his right. He was signing documents with his left hand, and so he must be left-handed.

When Ibrahim Jamaa's substitute took two steps to the edge of his desk and spoke to Sheila, he ran one of his long index fingers over the shoulder cradle of the telephone and along the thin neck of a desk lamp. For a left-handed person, those items are on the wrong side of the desk.

If he prefers to speak on the telephone and write while doing so (hence the shoulder cradle), the telephone would be on the other side of the desk so that the receiver could rest on his right shoulder while he wrote with his left hand. If there is any doubt about this logic, it is dispelled by the position of the desk lamp. It's on the same, or wrong, side of the desk.

26 Murder at 12 Carnavon

Honey has found the contradiction, she thinks, the crack in the carefully crafted defense that she needs to return the jury to rationality. What is it?

As Honey states, to herself and to Marion, the task she has is to point out a discrepancy in the seemingly precise case that Roland has built, so that the jury will focus on the issue at hand. If she can show that at least one of these ever-so-carefully verified details is inconsistent, then perhaps the jurors will reconsider their position.

There's no compelling reason to suspect the waitress of collusion in spilling the ketchup to give Barnett a reason to go home at midday. After all, waitresses do spill things. Besides, if it were a contrived spill, it would more likely have been coffee. Still, the weakness is in the spilled ketchup. During his testimony, Barnett held out his left leg to show where the ketchup had fallen. He then very carefully told the jury that he remembered being stuck with the pin by the tailor, right where the ketchup was still on his sock.

Anyone who has ever paid attention when pant cuffs are being measured and marked, especially by a professional tailor, would notice that the tailor always measures just one leg – the *right* leg. The little tailor, who would of course have been performing profession-ally, must have seen the ketchup on the right sock, whether or not he really stuck it with a pin.

This tiny point is precisely what Honey needs as a wedge.

27   The Case of Queen Isabella's Gift
Why has Geoff Dilley concluded that Vicar Titteridge has stolen the pair of candelabra?

Even though the vicar is a clear suspect, his story that a visitor to Evensong hid in the church is entirely plausible. But the story breaks down over the electric lights. Geoff's visit to St. Dunstan's-by-the-Water takes place during the day. Chief Inspector Peddelley-Spens, during his tirade, said that the prime minister of Portugal was com-ing in "this afternoon" and that he wanted Geoff back "before tea." It took Geoff an hour to get to St. Dunstan's, so it is daylight when he and the vicar enter the church.

They unlock the main door and enter. The church is dark and the vicar turns on the lights, so lighting is necessary at all times, even daytime, to function in the church. Because the vicar asks Geoff to exit by the main door so they can turn the lights out and lock up, the only light switches must be at that door.

If the vicar entered that morning by the back emergency door (as usual) and looked up (which was unusual), would he have been able to see that the candelabra were missing without first going to the back of the church and turning on the lights? The candelabra, after all, were placed so high that even with a step stool and an extended candlelighter they were difficult to light. It is far more likely that the vicar already knew they were missing.

It is interesting to note that Geoff was also very much aware that the conflict between Edward II and his queen, Isabella, was so intense that by 1326, six years after the dedication of St. Dunstan's, it had degenerated into civil war or, depending on one's point of view, a legitimate revolution. It's quite possible that in 1320 they may not have attended a dedication together.

George IV became Prince Regent in 1810. His father, by this time, was reported to be having animated conversations with a tree in the Great Park at Windsor, thinking it was Frederick the Great.

28   Quite Possibly, the Annual Meeting of the Ambiguity Society

When will the next annual meeting be held?

Bonnie must assume that none of the members are telling her the exact truth; yet she must take their answers at face value for her calculations. If she does that, she will find that every date but one in the month of May appears at least two, sometimes three times, when all the answers are considered, thus representing the nature of the Ambiguity Society.

Sally's first answer specifies a date *after* the thirteenth of the month. Her second specifies a date *before* the thirteenth. Thus every day is accounted for at least once except the thirteenth.

Karen Di Creche's answer adds the thirteenth along with every other odd-numbered date, and Julio's answer specifies every date of the month except May 4, 9, 16, and 25. Thus, every date in the month is mentioned at least two or three times (thereby establishing further ambiguity), except for May 4 and 16.

The very first response, the one from Bruno Steubens, specifies that the meeting will be held on the middle of the month just like this year. The middle of the month of May is the sixteenth, which means that date, too, has two answers. Therefore the only single, unambiguous choice of date is May 4.

29   The Case of the Missing Body

How does Lesley Simpson know that the skeleton was dumped into the trench last night?

Lesley Simpson could see that at the point in the trench where the skeleton was found, the earth was being excavated for the very first time as the trench was being dug. Had someone buried the body of Mrs. Vincent Gene there three years ago, the earth would have been disturbed by that excavation. However, what Sergeant Palmer pointed out to Lesley was a skeleton lying in earth that was still in its natural layers. It is entirely likely that this earth hadn't been disturbed since the last glacier passed through.

Therefore, the skeleton of Mrs. Gene must have been brought to the trench from elsewhere, dropped in, and then covered with loose earth for the backhoe operator to find the next day. If Vincent Gene is charged, it will likely be Lesley Simpson's argument that he is being framed by someone who put the body in the trench in an attempt to make it appear as though she had been buried there some time before.

30   The Case of the Marigold Trophy

Why does Janice Sant think the Palgrave Horticultural Society could lose its most prized possession?

Janice has been reading back issues of *The Daily Enterprise* on microfilm. She has available issues from 1903, 1904 and 1905. When Eugene Weller tells her it is closing time she is looking at a date in March. Since she has been reading carefully and in sequence for four hours (from five to nine without taking a break) and since she can cover five months of issues in an hour, the March she is looking at must be March 1904, the year the trophy was awarded to Maribeth Tooch. (She has covered twenty months; all of 1905 plus nine months of 1904 minus an October for either year. This would not work out if she had started with 1903 and worked forward in sequence.)

The date she is looking at is March 3. According to the article, Curragh O'Malley's horse ran down Ezra Templeton on March 2. On the same day a week earlier, it struck Maribeth Tooch just after she had seeded her marigolds. In three out of four years, the date of the same day a week earlier would have been February 23, the planting date for marigold seeds according to the contest rules, but 1904 is a leap year (any year divisible by four); therefore the date she was struck, *and* the date on which she seeded her marigolds for the contest, was February 24. The Grand Champion Marigold exhibitor of the 1904 Albion Agricultural Exhibition broke the rules!

31 The Coffee Break That Wasn't
What offense has Lennie detected at the Eat 'n' Run and how has she done it?

What Lennie is attempting to determine is whether she got a fresh cup of coffee or whether the waitress simply took out the plastic housefly and returned with the same cup of coffee. That's why she tasted the coffee with her little finger. She must have put sugar in the original cupful. When she tasted coffee from the "new" cup it must have been sweet, causing her to conclude the worst.

32 Who Shot the Clerk at Honest Orville's?
Of the several elements in the case that Mary and Caroline can present to evoke "reasonable doubt," there is one that stands out just a bit. What is that one?

Certainly the missing weapon is one element on which Mary and Caroline will undoubtedly lean, but their strongest point is likely a simple matter of physics. The time is pre-Christmas, close enough to the day itself for the Christmas shopping rush. The two young ladies were wearing coats, and Caroline made note of the overheated police station. Therefore, this is Christmas time in the northern hemisphere, so that by 8:40 p.m. it will be fully dark outside. If Honest Orville's sign has around fifty thousand bulbs, as the discussion reveals, then the area where the shooting took place will have a great deal of bright artificial light. However, if the shooting took place well out on the sidewalk, under the big sign, Kee Park would have been *backlit*. It would have been extremely difficult, therefore, to make out his face, if not impossible. Given that the patrolman-witness had to run across a wide, busy street to nab Kee Park and Mr. Sung, who were in a crowd, and had to stop traffic to do so (which would inevitably mean taking his eyes off the suspects), the two law students may well choose to press the witness on the issue of making a positive identification in, say, a lineup. He's not likely to succeed without reasonable doubt.

33   Speed Checked by Radar
What has made Fran Singleton ninety-nine percent sure that things are normal in the Internal Revenue Service building?

This was certainly not an easy decision for Fran to make. If there is something wrong, some threat in the building, then she will be held liable for failing to act. Yet to rush the building with the E.R. team could be disastrous for several reasons. Even for her to go in, with or without Constable Gold, could complicate things, too. And both choices attract lots of attention and would alert the crazies.

It behooved Fran to weigh the situation carefully, which is just what she did. Given what she learned from Constable Gold about the likely type of individual it was who was walking to and from the annex building, and given that it was very close to 4:30 p.m. on a Friday afternoon, she believes that in moving quickly, this possible "grunt" was behaving normally.

If it were likely that he was returning to a difficult situation, at least one that he couldn't leave by 4:30 p.m., he would probably have moved more slowly or deliberately. Quite likely the sight of a speeder being caught would have merited a longer look, too. He might even have tried to send a signal of some sort to the two police officers.

All this, however, is meaningless if the young man walking to the annex building is not a regular employee, but one of a group that has taken over the building, and who has been sent to the annex to further the appearance of normality. But one action of his signaled to Fran that he is a regular employee, and one familiar with the place. He not only anticipated the locked slab door while walking up the steps, he selected the right key from a large ring of keys and unlocked the door in a single motion. All his actions indicated that he has done this many times before. A "plant" would have been less automatic at some point in the procedure.

34 Where to Send "This Stuff Here"
Where and to whom will Sue Hageman send the guitar?

In the LAME Room, there are four cartons, each with items to go to four different players. Sue has to identify which item goes to which player and then arrange to send it to the airport of the appropriate city.

The former holder of Sue's job (now with the Glasgow Rangers) says that Nodl will have the names and addresses in the brown envelope she is carrying, however unorthodox they may seem. The names are Tino Savi, Giovanni Moro, and Gino Bellissime. Iago Cassini's name must be on one of the items already: the photography bag. The four cities are Turin (where the skis go), Naples, Milan, and Capri (where the chess sets go).

Iago Cassini gets the photography bag. Tino Savi does not ski, so he gets neither the skis nor the photography bag. Tino Savi does not live in Naples (he visited there) or Turin (where the skis are being sent). Since he does not live in Milan (where Gino Bellissime has a business with his wife), Tino Savi is from Capri and therefore gets the chess sets.

Giovanni Moro does not live in Naples or Milan (or Capri), so he must be from Turin, where the skis go. Since Gino lives in Milan, Iago Cassini must be from Naples. The remaining item of the four must be the guitar, which then goes to Gino Bellissime, or to his wife, in Milan.

35   A Witness in the Park
What has led Mary Blair to this conviction?

The season must be autumn, for Mary Blair's shoes leave prints in the frosty grass. Alicia Bell says there are leaves falling. Yet it must still be early autumn, for Mary notes that the ground was still too soft to walk on in high heels.

Anyone who gets up early enough on crisp but sunny autumn days, when the temperature is close to freezing, has seen the frost on the grass sparkling in the sunlight. However, particularly in early fall, that sparkle disappears within two to three hours of sunrise at the latest as the earth warms.

Alicia Bell was doing fine with her story about Ron Minaker digging flower bulbs out of Jack Atkin's flower bed until she mentioned the footprints in the frosty grass. It's quite possible that two days ago when the alleged digging took place, the weather was identical to the weather on the day Mary and Alicia met. And it's quite possible that Alicia could have been concealed just over the brow of a knoll behind the flower bed in question. But she couldn't have stood there until at least ten o'clock for the park gates are locked until then. By that time, in early fall, the frost on the grass has long melted away in the sunlight.

It appears that Alicia Bell was enjoying her story so much that she went too far.

36   An Urgent Security Matter at the U.N.

How has Ambassador Haruna manipulated the seating arrangement? And why does Chris want to check the security clearance for delegate Cresawana?

There are to be eight people at the table in the Singapore Room: Ambassador Manamoto and Bjarni Benediktsson, who are chair and vice-chair; General Nardone, Bishop Leoni, and Dr. Perez from one delegation; Ambassador Haruna, Ms. Gestido, and Mr. Cresawana from the other. Chris and Paul Fogolin can begin the seating arrangements knowing that the delegations have to be intermingled, and knowing that the heads of delegations will sit beside the chair, Ambassador Manamoto.

However, Ambassador Haruna has manipulated the seating. He has accomplished this by requesting that Ms. Gestido, of his delegation, be immediately beside him. (It makes no difference whether she is on his right or his left; by extension, therefore, Haruna can be either on Manamoto's right or left; the manipulation works in either direction at this round table. For purposes of description here, assume that Haruna is on the left, with Ms. Gestido to the immediate left of him.) Because of Ambassador Manamoto's intermingling condition, Mr. Cresawana cannot sit to her left in turn, and she does not want to sit beside Bishop Leoni, so only Benediktsson or Dr. Perez can sit there.

Ambassador Haruna apparently knows that Dr. Perez will not sit beside Gestido, so Bjarni Benediktsson must then be the one next to Ms. Gestido. To Benediktsson's left will be Dr. Perez because Haruna knows she won't sit beside Leoni or Nardone. Then to her left, in order, will be Mr. Cresawana, then Bishop Leoni, then General Nardone, as the circle goes back to Ambassador Manamoto.

This is the only seating arrangement that is possible if all the diplomats' requests are to be honored. And it has been arranged principally by Ambassador Haruna. Whether or not he has help from others (like Dr. Perez) we cannot be sure. All we can be sure of is that he has manipulated the seating arrangement with only one simple request: that Ms. Gestido be seated beside him. And his reason for the request is entirely valid and reasonable, too.

What is achieved by the manipulation is getting Mr. Cresawana immediately beside Bishop Leoni. Since Leoni is the suspect target, and Cresawana is new, it is only natural for the Fogolin brothers to suspect him.